Puerto Rico City

◆

David R. Martin

This book is a work of fiction. Names, characters, places and incidents either are products of the author's imagination or are used fictitiously. Any real or historical events serve only as a backdrop for a fictitious story. Any resemblance to actual events or locales or persons, living or dead, is entirely coincidental.

Copyright © 2012 David R. Martin

All rights reserved.

ISBN-10: 0-615-59361-5

ISBN-13: 978-0-615-59361-6

For information about special discounts for bulk purchases, please contact Puerto Rico City, LLC, 5200 Peachtree Road, Suite 3116, Atlanta, GA 30341, Tel. (877) 243-3462 or novel@puertoricocity.com.

DEDICATION

To my son, an entertainer

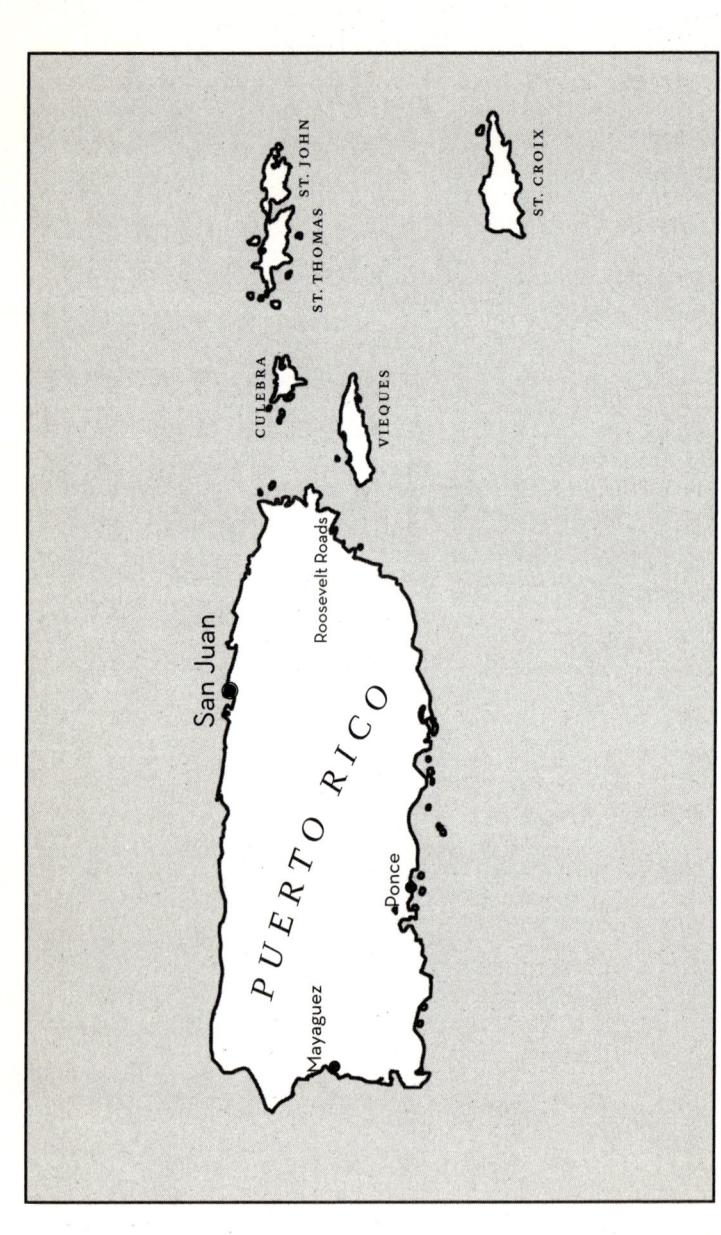

Table of Contents

ACKNOWLEDGMENTS i
1 Puerto Rico City 3
2 Roosevelt Roads 14
3 Lino Mendoza 17
4 Aaron Getz 24
5 Reed Savage 29
6 Wen Kashing 35
7 Sergei Rubelkov 40
8 Daisy Youngluck 45
9 Krysha 50
10 Diosa 58
11 Pocket Change 67
12 The Value of Real 75
13 No Second Chance 85
14 The Top-Up 91
15 The Bidders 98
16 Getzing Money 107
17 La Conquista 113
18 The Girasol 118
19 Reconquista Ltd. 121
20 The Auction 126
21 A Martínez 131
22 Duopoly 135
23 The Award 139
24 The Team 143
25 The Government 151
26 Madame Secretary 158
27 Okinawa 163
28 The Borinquen Trust 171
29 Puerto Rico Air 179
30 Stateside Crucible 186
31 The City 194
32 Statehood 199
ABOUT THE AUTHOR 201

"And as natural selection works solely by and for the good of each being, all corporeal and mental endowments will tend to progress towards perfection." Charles Darwin, *The Origin of the Species (*1859).

"In the social production of their existence, men inevitably enter into definite relations, which are independent of their will…" Karl Marx, *A Contribution to the Critique of Political Economy* (1859).

"What is man? The point I want to make now is that all attempts to answer that question before 1859 are worthless and that we will be better off if we ignore them completely." George Gaylord Simpson (1966)

ACKNOWLEDGMENTS

I want to thank my father Manuel Martínez-Maldonado, author of *El Vuelo del Dragón* and *Isla Verde (El Chevy Azúl)*, for his sage advice and editorial recommendations. I also want to thank the other lasting and memorable voices of encouragement to pursue the craft of writing, especially Alan Lelchuk, Howell Chickering, David Sofield, John Cameron, the late Antonio Benítez-Rojo and the late Rust Hills, former fiction editor of *Esquire* magazine, whose letter of encouragement many years ago kept a small flame burning inside of me.

1 PUERTO RICO CITY

♦

In different times, Lino Mendoza would have instantly reframed the onslaught by the U.S. Navy as a repugnant symbol of American imperialism. But he had been too busy on deals for investment banks and other status-conscious clients at Ashton & Cavendish, one of New York City's top law firms. Lino started at the firm after graduating from Yale and clerking for a federal judge in Manhattan. Lino observed events in Puerto Rico with fragmented attention and a general sense that, in the grand scheme of the world's business, Puerto Rico was a coincidental, but minor detail of his past. Still, he casually followed news about the island.

Lino's rise to partnership at Ashton & Cavendish had not been without its travails, mostly endured in secrecy. Accent elimination classes, sartorial studies, impulse control, and background revisionism started during law school. Even though his left knee flared up in cold or humid days, he got rid of the cane. He shaved off his moustache. Despite his social conversations to the contrary, Lino had not really grown up in a penthouse on Ashford Avenue in Condado. He had never insisted on working sleeve buttons for his suit jackets or a silk handkerchief in his breast pocket. His family had not really given him his first car as a gift.

He had stolen it, a Chevrolet Camaro, from an Hato Rey movie theater parking lot. Lino knew that he had to defend it. Physical force, not law, protects stolen property. Ask any American. He used a razor knife – a double-sided razor blade available in any grocery store, wedged onto one end of a stick. It was dark and it was necessary. The odds were roughly even. Lino and his challenger were both armed. While Lino felt he had made solid contact, he never really saw his opponent's face or the wound. New blue paint, shiny alloy rims, and the Camaro was Lino's. After the Camaro, Lino bought a Glock 17 handgun and kept it under the driver's seat. He had used it twice.

Neither the hundreds of contract cases that he studied at Yale, nor the thousands of hours of negotiations he had witnessed as a corporate lawyer could have taught him the vital lessons that he had learned during his youth from committing unpunished crimes. Paramount among these was keeping certain information to oneself. He witnessed scores of Ivy League wunderkinds disappear into professional oblivion for violating this basic tenet.

The money was good at Ashton & Cavendish — enough to buy an apartment in Manhattan's Carnegie Hill area. Yet the real wealth flowed to those doing the deals — the CEOs with chronic ego attacks who needed just one more acquisition for "increased synergies." Allaying their status anxiety meant having more employees to replace with offshore workers at a fraction of the cost. Then, after casting off the expensive bodies, the executioners held scripted press conferences, blaming high taxes and overregulation for the layoffs and the nation's economic woes. This elegant cover story dovetailed beautifully with political rhetoric. Captains of industry handed paper currency to pole dancers of policymaking, then followed the invitations to campaign dinners, lunches and political favors that served as deposits for future withdrawal.

The average high-precision factory worker in China earned sixteen percent of an American counterpart. Even if the U.S. government lowered corporate taxes to zero, going offshore was still far more profitable. The unsparing laws of supply and demand blurred the distinction between slavery and employment. Indeed, it was less expensive and complicated to pay the going hourly rate for a human being, who was hypothetically free to quit at any time, than to own and control that person outright. Deal after deal conveyed these facts to Lino with brutal clarity.

Still in his mid-thirties, Lino was single but never lonely. His favorite prospecting grounds were the clothing stores on Broadway in Greenwich Village. "Multinational" women, as Lino thought of them, worked or shopped in these places. They surpassed the most richly paid Hollywood talent. The most beautiful women in the world did not appear in movies or magazines. They worked and shopped in New York City boutiques. They went about their lives knowing their allure, but few had the ambition and ovaries to fully exploit it. With women, Lino maintained the playful and mocking detachment that his mother taught him to have. During his childhood, Lino watched his mother mercilessly shed dozens of overeager lovers. With this guiding principle, Lino had no broken heart in his future.

Puerto Rico City

Lino strategically planned his leisure time away from the firm. As soon as a deal closed, he bought airplane tickets and left with one of several girlfriends. That way, the risk of interruption was minimized during three to five-day absences. Las Vegas became a regular destination. Flights to and from Laguardia and JFK were frequent. Just as in New York, once in Las Vegas, he seldom needed a car. He avoided the wasted time and hassle of driving. A fifteen-minute cab ride and he was on the Strip. Over several years, he sampled almost every hotel from The Wynn to Mandalay Bay.

He spoke with his mother Nereida from time to time, but nearly always from his apartment or away from his office. He tried to avoid speaking Spanish in the law firm, even with staff who were visibly bilingual and Hispanic. There are very few advantages to wearing one's ethnicity on one's sleeve. He went several years without visiting Puerto Rico, until one winter after much of New York City had been snowed in. Lino helped close a merger, then took the next flight.

Lino checked in at The Gallery Inn on Norzagaray Street in Old San Juan. It was an upscale boutique hotel catering mostly to stateside American and European travelers, where Lino would probably not be recognized. The next day, he visited his mother in Miramar. She was recently retired but still attractive. Puerto Rican women age well. In earlier years, she had had many suitors. Several years ago, Lino had bought Nereida a two-story home.

Nereida had graduated at the top of her class at the University of Puerto Rico Law School and then passed the bar with the highest score, attainments that, ironically, caused her to be shunned by the male-dominated law firms in San Juan. Several law review articles she had written against "the American occupation" were also unhelpful to a mainstream legal career. In addition, she had been married briefly to Lino's father, Santiago Mendoza, once a close advisor to Juan Carlos Peña, the perennial gubernatorial candidate for the Puerto Rico National Independence Party. When Lino was two, Santiago died in a mysterious automobile accident, which some believed had been orchestrated by the Central Intelligence Agency. Puerto Rican nationalists and the CIA were not exactly great bedfellows.

After her husband's death, Nereida was tasked with keeping control of Lino and finding appropriate punishments for other youth scoundrels as a municipal court judge. Such was the respect for her legal acumen, however, that judges from the superior courts and even the Puerto Rico Supreme Court would privately call her in her modest chambers for all manner of legal opinions, ranging from complex questions on search-and-seizure to federal preemption.

As customary, when they were together, Lino and Nereida mostly communicated non-verbally. She served rice, sweet plantains and steak. Lino ate everything on his plate. This meant he loved her and she him.

As he left, Lino told Nereida in Spanish: "Remember, I'm not here."

There were literally hundreds of obligatory visits and phone calls Lino would have to make if his presence were known. When he left for Yale, the local papers published the news. Lino disappeared into his studies, and the island media inquiries for updates trailed off until eventually they stopped. Nevertheless, there were still many friends, professors, former classmates, and general onlookers who would remember him. Lino spent the next four days touring the island in a rented Ford SUV. He started his drive wearing a Los Angeles Dodgers baseball cap, Bulgari sunglasses, frayed jeans, flip flops, and a dark green Ralph Lauren polo shirt. Puerto Rican? Nuyorican? Gringo?

As Lino drove, the sunny weather was impeccable in the mid 80s. A purifying breeze blew steadily from the coast. He contrasted this with a visit to Las Vegas the year before when snow fell, forcing him and his date indoors all day – not, however, the worst of fates.

Puerto Rico beaches were spectacular but sporadically littered with trash. The casinos were microscopic by Las Vegas and Atlantic City standards. The maximum bet limits were laughably low. There was little or nonexistent live entertainment. An unknown salsa band at a hotel bar was often the most significant event. Cars congested the streets. Walking outside to another hotel could be jarring as their horns honked and high beams flashed in your face. Prices were similar to New York and Las Vegas: ten dollars for a six-ounce rum and Coke, forty dollars for a five-ounce filet. Even then, the hotels and casinos were buzzing with stateside visitors. Gamblers were betting the maximum $3,000 per play at the tables.

He remembered the redeye flights from Las Vegas to New York, packed from stem to stern with wired-in passengers like him, stressing over their laptops to preserve their disposable income. They had temporarily escaped the pressures and provocations of face-to-face office meetings and could enjoy, for a few days, the luxury of proofreading a response through some form of digital leash. *New Yorkers returning from a freezing Las Vegas on a five-hour flight in February?* – Lino thought to himself.

In Manhattan, he would occasionally see a lifeless billboard advertisement for Puerto Rico. Seldom did Lino see promotions for the island on television. He read somewhere that Puerto Rico had about 13,000 hotel rooms. He read somewhere else that Hawaii had 45,000 rooms. He had been to the Hawaiian islands, which had been "annexed" as a U.S. territory in 1898— the same year that the Puerto Rican islands, including Vieques, Culebra and Mona, had been acquired by the U.S. as booty from the Spanish-American War. Hawaii was a thousand miles farther from the West Coast than Puerto Rico was from the East Coast. And the East Coast had more people. Also, he had trouble finding a sand-bottom beach in Oahu and the Big Island. The best advice to avoid cutting your feet on the sharp underwater rocks and coral in Waikiki was to wear rubber-soled wading shoes. In contrast, sand-bottom beaches were the rule in Puerto Rico.

However, the pharmaceutical industry, not its tourist sites, was Puerto Rico's claim to economic fame.

A federal tax exemption, known as Section 936 of the U.S. Internal Revenue Code, had drawn U.S. pharmaceutical companies and other manufacturers to the U.S. island territory. In the 1990s Congress pulled the plug on 936, and the federal tax break completely phased out by the end of 2005. Had it not been for the dual benefit of lower wages and the tax exemption, big pharma and other manufacturers had little reason to be in Puerto Rico. Indeed, when 936 started to burn out, companies began leaving in droves. Puerto Rico's policy makers harbored illusions of anointing the island as a knowledge-based mecca of technology and manufacturing. But in his work as a corporate lawyer, Lino had seen these industries digitized or offshored to places with more tech-minded traditions and far lower wages.

With the sweet taste of his mother's plantains still in his mouth, Lino headed west towards Rincón, a small town leading to a hilly sand and rock peninsula well-known to veteran surfers and their scenic girlfriends. He spent the night at El Tamboo guesthouse. He became playful with a waitress from a neighboring restaurant. The next day, he took her home to San Sebastián, then drove, by himself, south through Mayagüez, then San Germán and Yauco. He continued eastward to Ponce, then drove to Humacao taking the winding road up the mountains and the east coast on Route 3. When the road poked out along the shore, he could see the island of Vieques beyond a veil of blue mist in the distance.

The newspaper and magazine reports about the protests five years ago that stopped the bombings on Vieques came to Lino's mind. He approached the entrance to Roosevelt Roads, the former U.S. naval base. He wanted to see it. Two Puerto Rican security guards wearing black caps and blue shirts manned the checkpoint. He drove up and asked in English for permission to enter. It was noxious to his anti-imperialist sentiments of yore, but the truth was that if you wanted an extra volt of attention in Puerto Rico, you spoke English. However, when he said that he did not have U.S. military identification, the security guards said no. He had never entered this naval base. It occurred to him that most Puerto Ricans also had never set foot on this land either. In fact, for the overwhelming majority of the Puerto Rican population, the thirteen-square miles of coastal land acquired by the U.S. Navy some 67 years ago in the municipalities of Ceiba and Naguabo did not, for practical purposes, even exist.

This place needed a new name.

2 ROOSEVELT ROADS

♦

Firing practice and amphibious assaults by the U.S. Navy had occurred for decades. Destroyers, frigates, landing craft, fighter jets, and helicopters departed from Roosevelt Roads. Seven miles offshore to the southeast of Roosevelt Roads was the twenty-mile-long island target of Vieques. The Vieques population of about 9,000 was restricted to a crooked western swath, bounded by the north and south coasts, covering about one-third of the island. Before the U.S. Navy bought the other two-thirds in 1941 as part of the creation of the Roosevelt Roads, Vieques had been the home of sugarcane plantations and refineries. Where spared by exploding ordnance, the beaches are magnificent. Shiny brown wild horses roam the grassy fields. The vegetation varies from exotic tropical flowers to desert cacti.

Aside from fishing, the Puerto Ricans living on Vieques, known as *viequenses*, had few ways to distract themselves from the jolt of gunfire, explosions and the thunder of military engines at sea and in the sky. Puerto Rican nationalist groups had been active from time to time against "the American occupation." In 1950, two nationalists attempted to assassinate President Harry S. Truman as he was leaving Blair House in Washington, D.C. In 1954, pro-independence radicals, including the infamous Lolita Lebrón, wounded five members of the U.S. Congress with automatic weapons during a session of the House of Representatives. In 1981, another rebel faction, the Macheteros, destroyed ten attack aircraft at the Air National Guard Base in San Juan. Protests against the navy's use of Vieques and its smaller sister island of Culebra had been happening since the 1970s, but they only started to gather mainstream support in 1999 when a stray bomb killed a local civilian security guard on Vieques.

In 2003, as a result of continuing protests, the navy stopped the exercises on Vieques. Puerto Ricans celebrated. Then, in 2004, the U.S. Department of Defense decided to close the base. Roosevelt Roads had been one of the U.S.'s largest naval bases and home of the U.S. Naval Forces Southern Command. The base had an airport with two runways, one longer than the runway of San Juan's main international airport. There were reports that the government of Puerto Rico practically got on its knees, begging for the U.S. to keep the base open. Thousands of naval personnel left, and a skeleton crew of contractors was kept to conduct maintenance. Hundreds and millions of dollars were lost each year from the island's economy. Two Puerto Rico government administrations batted about plans for the base. Political bickering and inertia set in.

With naval ships gone and the guns silenced, Roosevelt Roads and Vieques quietly faced each other across the seven-mile passage of blue and turquoise water. Puerto Rico's economy bled and withered. Unofficial estimates of unemployment, usually the most accurate, were over 20 percent.

3 LINO MENDOZA

♦

Nobody likes to get pushed around. Nobody. It is human nature to take control, be top dog, attain escape velocity, and maybe one day – as said somewhere in *The Great Gatsby* – sit cool and pretty above the hot struggles of the poor.

He was no different, except, perhaps, that he had an elephantine memory and harbored huge grudges. He started in the streets of Santurce, Puerto Rico, near bus stop number eight on Ponce de León Avenue. He liked American football, a game that he first saw in a stolen cable TV signal from the Virgin Islands. He had a taste for girls with cinnamon-colored skin, the kind that swayed past him on sidewalks and plazas in cities and towns around the island. He had a lighter complexion, dark hair, a sinewy physique. The movements of his hands and arms were agile and, precise. He walked quickly. His green eyes worked well below a protruding brow. When needed, he could be ruthlessly crude and revolting. He was able to spit slimy, enveloping snot masses across two street lanes. Before he graduated to a razor knife, then a Glock 17 handgun and then undercover guards, his ability to spit such large distances earned him undeniable fear and respect. Few embarrassments and taunts were more thorough and stigmatizing than being plastered by his greenish, gelatinous launchings from 20 feet away. Someone once floated the nickname "Cobra," but he splattered down the few who dared to utter this term within snot shot.

School, whenever he decided to go, was mostly for stealing lunch money and lifting skirts on cinnamon thighs. Depending on the stakes, he would oscillate from charming to repulsive. He earned his first lesson in timed diplomacy one day when he and eight of his "dogs" got caught inside of a house in a nice neighborhood. They were unplugging appliances and fancy visual and sound systems.

"Yes, officer, anything to help you. If I could just call my mother. I think I see her outside," he said in Spanish.

At that stage of his life, Lino knew only two facts about Puerto Rico's legal system. First, there was no death penalty. Second, there was a strict law enforcement policy not to shoot fourteen year olds for petty burglaries. So he made a run for it. He left his crew behind and disappeared through Hato Rey's side streets and alleys. As memories faded and after he sharpened his debating and Q&A skills against his mother's withering logic and interrogations, he hit the streets again.

While he neglected school, Lino learned that words, numbers, and alliances were useful. And this awareness planted a helpful seed of doubt to crosscheck his senses. When he was in high school, Lino Mendoza scraped together enough Nuyoricans (Puerto Ricans who had lived in New York or New Jersey) to form an American football team for his school, Mariela Merced. Lino's team played with second and third-hand defective equipment. The team did not have a coach on the sidelines. They played against the English-speaking private schools in San Juan. His team did not win a single game.

When it was clear that the prospect of winning was an illusion, Lino orchestrated gang-style hits on opposing players. The most effective takedowns involved players who did not even have the ball. After several expulsions by the referees, word got around. Then, of course, there was payback. Commonwealth High School offensive lineman Bob Tutton was known in the league as Two Ton. At six-foot-five and 270 pounds, he was the largest and most agile player in the history of Puerto Rican high school football. Two Ton knew the hit was coming. On the snap of the ball, Two Ton disregarded his blocking assignment and charged straight at Lino in the defensive backfield. Lino tried to dodge him, but Two Ton wrenched Lino up by the ankle and jacked him off the grass. Lino's left knee was never quite the same again. He tried launching a missile of snot at Two Ton, but it got caught in Lino's facemask. Both sides of the field started at each other, but at the sight of the first razor knife, the private school guys stopped, retreated and left in nice cars legally registered in their names.

Lino returned to school three weeks later with a walking cane.

"Lino, what happened?" his math teacher asked.

"A horse bit me." Lino said with a smirk. There was laughter.

Defiant leadership earned him passing grades in classes that he did not even attend. A fair description of Lino's early academic efforts was that he did half of his assignments but remembered nearly all of what he learned. He pivoted between Spanish and English on a dime. He read quickly. In his senior year, he sat for the Puerto Rico counterpart of the SAT and missed only two questions.

The University of Puerto Rico accepted him as a freshman. Tuition was five dollars a credit — about $120 a year for a full course load of classes. A student maintaining a B average paid nothing. Lino took political science courses and never paid a cent for his classes. Even though he did not really need one, he used an assortment of walking canes, each with a different handle design. He grew a moustache.

Like several of his professors, Lino acquired a keen interest in Karl Marx, Che Guevara and Fidel Castro. To add a romantic gloss to a deterministic ideology, he committed to memory poetic passages of Gabriel García Márquez's *One Hundred Years of Solitude*. Despite his insouciant nature, Lino found it exceedingly difficult to make light of the final ominous pronouncement, almost a one-size-fits-all Buddhist koan for humanity – that races condemned to a hundred years of solitude did not get a second chance on Earth.

He graduated with honors in political science, but continued living on the Río Piedras campus with a series of girlfriends who were still students. Although no longer officially enrolled, Lino dropped in on undergraduate political science classes. He was a vigorous participant. Lino would rise to his feet with the help of the unnecessary cane for effect. He started with simple questions, then escalated from there until he crested into rousing dialectical speeches calling for Puerto Rico independence and the end of capitalism. Oratorically flourished female students slipped their phone numbers into Lino's shirt pocket.

A year on, the University announced a tuition increase from five dollars per credit to ten dollars ($240 per year). Lino led a student strike, shutting down the entire campus. Television stations gave him regular interviews. Two island newspapers, competing for the largest circulation, bid against each other for Lino to become a regular columnist. After a few years, Lino netted $150,000, socialized evenly between both newspapers. When the University dropped its plan to raise tuition, Lino initially envisioned a career as a politician.

However, with an investment account at Merrill Lynch, his anti-capitalist sentiments waned. *This money thing, it's not so bad* – Lino thought to himself. He started buying *The Wall Street Journal* for five dollars a copy. *Small wonder why it was so expensive and difficult to learn about business in Puerto Rico.* As Lino read, it seemed that many people of consequence had gone to the same schools: Harvard, Yale, and Stanford, to name a few. He completed applications to law schools. Harvard and Stanford sent one-page rejection letters. Then, despite Lino's two arrests for disturbing the peace during student tuition protests, Yale Law School accepted him. Yearly tuition: $40,000. Lino wrote the check posthaste.

4 AARON GETZ

♦

Over the Atlantic, northwesterly, somewhere in the Tri-State area, another boy had grown up, two decades before Lino. He was a bottom-liner from the first day he sucked milk from a breast. He detested losing. Playing marbles or arguing over a seat on the subway, he usually got his way. Kids mocked him for being Jewish, but Aaron Getz had never seen the inside of a synagogue. And he would not be counted by the orthodoxy. His father, Jacob (actually Yaakov), had married Patricia Sullivan, a tough, laser-minded Irish-Catholic girl from Brooklyn. Shortly after Getz's first communion, his father disappeared one night after a poker game. The unofficial story was that Jacob had been winning, and winning big. Gambling debts are either paid or expire when the loser or winner dies.

Like his late father, Getz had a good head for numbers. But unlike his father, he knew when to cover his flanks and close off the openings that left him vulnerable. Getz did not learn these skills from anyone, and he often wondered from whence they came.

Getz played "flips" with his grade school classmates. Two guys stand across from each other and each flips a coin of equal value. One guy calls "odds" or "evens" as they both cover their coins on the back of their hands. If the caller said "odds" and the two coins were on different sides, the caller won the other guy's coin. The guy who didn't call got to see the caller's coin first. Getz seldom called the toss. He would flip his coin and secretly tilt it up vertically on the back of one hand while covering his coin with the other. When he saw the coin of the opponent, Getz would imperceptibly turn the coin to the opposite side of the call. He didn't do this all the time. For cheating to work, you can't win them all.

Getz applied this knowledge to other fields when he took a few community college courses in accounting. He bought two department store suits and started working for small brokerage firm in Brooklyn. Getz read the study guide in three days and passed his Series 7 securities exam on the first try. He quit community college and began selling "investments."

Getz tipped the security desk personnel to infiltrate upmarket assisted-living centers in Brooklyn and Queens. He knocked on the doors of each floor. The lonely and old are usually happy to talk to someone. In the 1970s and 80s, he sold "direct participation programs," also known as oil and gas limited partnerships. These investments started paying out immediately.

"See, you're making money already," he liked to tell his clients.

However, the partnership units seldom paid out more than their cost to the investor. When his clients wanted their money back, Getz responded: "Good investors are patient."

Patience kills. Most of Getz's clients were too old or sick to be patient. Some died. Others gave up. A few sued, but had to arbitrate in a broker-friendly forum. Nevertheless, his commissions more than offset the settlements and arbitration awards. Still, the earn rate was too slow, and Getz needed much, much more to end the cycle of female rejection followed by lonely masturbational retreats. Even in his twenties, Getz had the slight stoop of a middle-aged man and could never quite fill in a suit jacket, no matter how well-tailored. When walking with his splayed feet, he waddled. And most women standing barefoot were taller.

The timing, skill, and acumen that instinctively served him in business all but vanished at the sight of long, smooth legs, shapely hips and cleavage. But he did not lack persistence, and he aimed high in female attractiveness. Still, a kiss on the cheek was a major feat. A highly successful date, for him, typically ended with a friendly hug. To hedge against this diminished capacity, Getz tried to quantify in money his intermediations with the feminine. *Was there a positive correlation between the restaurant bill and her hotness? What happens if I intentionally spend less when she's more attractive?* This system, however, was fraught with ever-shifting considerations, risks and well-known unknowns – just the way it is supposed to be in order for a man to plunge headlong into the female vortex, risking blood and treasure to perpetuate the human species. Still, Getz returned to the solid touchstones of reason and analysis. He had read about giants of commerce and international moguls who suffered public humiliations and disfiguring financial amputations in divorce proceedings.

Hence, by the age of 30, Getz had cryogenically preserved enough sperm to procreate more children than Genghis Khan. Then he had a vasectomy. Pure reason. By 35, he had his own brokerage firm. By 42, he had offices on both coasts, staffed almost entirely by Jewish employees. They had to remind him constantly to give them days off for Passover, Rosh Hashanah, Yom Kippur, and their children's mitzvahs. Getz went from selling investments to making investments. His firm became a significant, albeit fleeting shareholder of various types of companies. Investment earnings paid for two jets and a yacht. But Getz could never hang on to a woman.

5 REED SAVAGE

♦

Across the American continent, in Los Angeles, a tall, lean, muscular fellow spent two teenage summers parking cars for restaurants on Sunset Boulevard. He approached the driver's side first and handed the man a claim check. He always noticed the inside of the man's jacket and whether he wore lace-up shoes or loafers. Then he swooped over to the passenger's side. With a clean hand and direct but appropriate eyes-on-eyes greeting, Reed Savage helped the lady out of the car. He trained himself not to look directly at her legs or breasts. He could assess these well enough through his keen peripheral vision.

His first self-taught lessons in statistics showed a high and predictable correspondence between distinctive jacket linings and lace-up men's dress shoes on one hand, and expensive cars and dazzling feminine company on the other.

Savage supplemented his tips with the change he found in car coin holders. He knew better than to steal all of the change. Only the risible bean counter would remember that he had exactly $4.85 in coins when he was missing a buck fifty.

Savage attributed his hunter's vision to being part Apache Native American on his mother's side. Except for his powerful black eyes, however, all traces of Native American physiognomy were buried in a classical white, athletic, six-foot-four build. By sitting next to the right people and seeing their oval answer marks, Savage improved his SAT scores enough to get into Williams College.

He coasted at Williams, playing rugby, drinking beer, smoking a joint here and there, dropping some acid once or twice. Maybe more than twice. He did well with the ladies. He took just enough "jock" courses, (geology, psychology, and applied art) to maintain an overall grade-point average high enough to get into Wharton Business School. Unless money was involved, few things pissed him off. He knew to overlook the small and keep his eye on the big payoffs.

The summer after his junior year in college, after Savage turned 21, he passed up an unpaid internship at a hedge fund in Greenwich, Connecticut, to work as an evening parking valet at The Wynn in Las Vegas. He spent the mornings playing blackjack at the Golden Nugget, Four Queens, Binion's, and other casinos in Old Vegas. These had lower minimum bets, dealers dealing cards from a shoe, and no automatic shuffler. Savage didn't count cards. It was too brain-intensive and time consuming, but he had a set of rules that worked.

The dealer had approximately a 51 percent chance of beating him on any given hand. However, he learned from an introductory statistics class (one of the few courses he took seriously), that the dealer's chances of beating him four times in a row (assuming everyone at the table played basic strategy and the same number of players stayed at the table) could be calculated thusly: .51 x. .51 x. .51 x .51 = 6.765201%. So, assuming the same number of players remained at the table, a dealer had something better than a 1 in 16 chance of winning four times in a row. Cheating by the house was not certain, but why take the chance? For Savage, the card magician in the Las Vegas Crazy Horse show at the MGM Grand was billionaire Kirk Kerkorian's gentle way of warning you about the phenomenal skills of card cheats.

So, if the dealer won four in row, Savage left the table. If the dealer was messy, that is, dropping cards, underpaying on buy-ins or payouts, Savage left the table. If the dealer dealt "seconds," meaning that the dealer drew two cards at the same time from the shoe, Savage left the table. If Savage's bet was large enough when "seconds" were dealt, he would kindly ask the dealer and then the pit boss, if that didn't work, to cancel the hand entirely. If the dealer was rude, he left the table. If the dealer was too nice, he left the table. If the dealer started banging the shoe up and down because cards were not easily coming out, Savage left the table. But, when the conditions were right and Savage stayed at the table, he deployed his unusually keen peripheral vision to catch a glimpse of the dealer's hole card when the dealer failed to keep it flat against the table.

If he doubled his money, Savage walked away and came back only after several days (or never at all) but always with a different look, less or more facial hair, a different hat, different sleeves, shorts instead of long pants.

After six weeks, he bought three tailored suits with silk burgundy lining. He wore lace-up Churchill English straight caps. He took home a little under $45,000 cash. The best way to hold cash? A rubber band and safe deposit boxes.

He breezed through Wharton in two years, got an offer for paid work at a hedge fund, but turned it down to nip casinos in Atlantic City, Biloxi, the Bahamas, the Dominican Republic, Puerto Rico, and Las Vegas. In about five months, Savage had netted more than $200,000.

One morning, while reading the *Las Vegas Sun*, Savage saw an ad in the business classifieds saying: "Native American tribe in Connecticut looking for start-up funds for casino. Provable Native American blood required."

The Arrowhead Casino was housed in a converted public elementary school in wooded area near the southwestern border of Connecticut. It started with college kids using fake IDs and gambling with mom and dad's money. Savage bought in with his $200,000. He had two partners, Billy Wildfoot and Chet Lighthorse. They knew next to nothing about business and much less about gambling. Savage invested in nicer bathrooms, prettier waitresses, a music and dance stage. He taught dealers how to win regularly six, seven and even eight times in a row. Any blackjack dealer sloppy enough to make his hole card visible was out in a jiffy. Savage ramped up the advertising. The casino started drawing adult players from Manhattan. Savage met no resistance for his proposal to add a hotel. In five years, the casino had a hotel with a thousand rooms. The property became The Deer Hunter Hotel & Casino.

Savage had started with a 20 percent interest, the same as his stated proportion of Apache blood. In ten years, with the help of Aaron Getz, his Apache blood content, as well as his interest in the Native American casino hotel resort, had grown to 100 percent. Wildfoot and Lighthorse had signed papers they did not understand. However, as Savage's well-paid do-nothing "consultants," they squawked not.

When Savage was in his early 40s, yearly profits from The Deer Hunter, now with 3,000 rooms, exceeded $100 million. Savage liked everything about the business except the Connecticut winters. He began taking regular trips during winter to the Dominican Republic and Puerto Rico.

6 WEN KASHING

♦

Wen Kashing grew up near the docks of Hong Kong harbor. At the age of ten, his mother Jia took him to find after-school work unloading cargo – mostly liquor. Wen saw the crates of Stolichnaya, Cutty Black, Rémy Martin, Bacardí, Tanqueray and Don Q and envisioned the world beyond as a menu of exotic choices. On paydays, however, sobering reality rained on his dreams to explore other lands. His mother Jia was a striking hourglass-shaped spa worker at the Velvet Sky Hotel in Kowloon City. She was used to being in command. Jia required that Wen turn over to her every Hong Kong dollar.

Wen had six siblings, none of which looked like him or like the other. He had no idea who his father was, and his mother told him: "Not important. He dead." Her dismissive attitude towards his genetic composition was echoed in Wen's hardscrabble neighborhood, where the identity of one's father was a question that you simply did not ask.

At twelve, Wen's frame began its vertical stretch. He outgrew his two older, reputed brothers by the time he was sixteen. He was six-foot-two, and taller than almost everyone he saw. His shoulders were broad and relaxed. He leaned back slightly when he walked. It seemed like the only men that were taller were those white visitors who spoke English.

After Jia could no longer meet Wen at eye level in her heels, Wen got the first urge to defy her. As foreign travel yearnings gnawed at his complicated family bonds, Wen started giving Jia only part of his earnings and saving the rest. He opened a savings account at Tai Sang Bank with five thousand Hong Kong dollars. He knew the exact balance at every moment thereafter. He developed an effective routine for saving money on his purchases:

"Seven Hong Kong for the coffee? I only have six…. Eighty for this shirt? Will you take seventy?"

Relaxed and tall, Wen looked down with a smile, bordering on a sneer and intimating the question: "Is this really going to break you?" Wen usually got the discount.

Wen had seen crewmen from the cargo ships playing Pai Gow poker on the tops of smaller shipping crates used to carry rum, mostly Don Q. They took turns being the dealer. The sums in Hong Kong dollars were relatively small, they complained, and word "Macau" kept rolling off the players' tongues. The game seemed simple enough: American poker with a Joker that can be used as an Ace or to complete a straight or flush. Wen still knew little about odds, but he could detect excitement or disappointment from the angle of an arm, a decibel change in a player's voice, the tilt of a head or back, the time it took for a player to make a bet, fidgeting. He started predicting correctly who would win. Not who had the best hand, but who would win. Who would live, however, was another question that Wen became expert at answering. Even over modest amounts, the bodies of dock workers would, now and then, be found floating in the Hong Kong harbor as barely recognizable fishmeal.

His success in these predictions spurred Wen to apply his senses more broadly. English and Cantonese were all around him, but the best dressed men spoke English. And they spoke English with a smooth, crafted flow, not by linking words in the jaunty, abrupt, metallic utterings he heard from many Asian-looking speakers.

There was a British-style pub, the Bulldog, a ten-minute walk from the docks that piped in European football as well as televised sessions of the British House of Commons. Wen began practicing a repertoire of phrases and expressions:

"I commend my honorable friend for his question."

"If someone is going to jump on the bandwagon, make sure it's still moving."

"Of course I understand the skepticism of the honorable gentleman."

"I think we should have a little bit of humility from someone who so utterly fails to grasp my point."

"What greater example could there be that this plan is working?"

Wen practiced his elocution and kept shaving off the top of his dockyard earnings until one day, approaching his eighteenth birthday, he had enough for a boat ride and trip to Macau. His English and impressive knowledge of liquor brands helped him land a job as a bartender at the Casa Real Casino. He worked his way up to a dealer and learned baccarat and blackjack. He began lending his tips to his fellow dealers for short-term loans at ten percent interest per week. His money grew to the point where he was able to buy a condo and a transcendently meaningful BMW. It soon became evident to Wen, however, that the greatest transcendental meaning accrued to those invisible owners and operators of the hotels and casinos that were mushrooming on the Macau peninsula and then, later, across the bridges in the Cotai district of Macau's Taipa Island.

7 SERGEI RUBELKOV

In 1991, when he was eleven, Sergei Rubelkov arrived with his parents in Tallinn, Estonia from Moscow. The Soviet Union had splintered away from Russia, which was adrift and rudderless. Estonia's economy was headed upward fast. Rubelkov's father worked on the finance end of a shipping firm and made enough for a luxury apartment for Rubelkov and his mom. However, there were too many rules, and people went to jail for breaking them. He watched his father filling out paperwork every few months in his study and saying aloud: "If I don't do this, I'll go to prison. Can you believe it? Prison?"

Rubelkov didn't have time for rules, and his parents indulged him. When he first found out how to start his dad's Audi sedan, he took it down the driveway and slammed it into a waste truck at the first intersection. *Was their sweet curly haired boy OK?* – was all that his parents wanted to know. Damage to the Audi was immaterial.

As his parent's only child, Rubelkov could do no wrong. In anyone's book, he was also quite clever. He started playing chess at a local chess club and obtained a 2200 rating by age twelve. The chess club supervisor recommended him for formal instruction, but Rubelkov was unenthusiastic. Tech gadgets drew his fancy. His private school offered computer courses, which he pursued on his own late into the night in his bedroom. He soon tired of programming his own video games, which promised only fleeting, penny-caliber victories. He became interested in more useful tools and devices. Rubelkov started hacking into nearby computers appearing wirelessly within range, mostly in neighboring units of his parents' upscale apartment complex.

Lurking in the digital ether, he drew back the veil of ancient myths. People usually had much more, or far less, than they claimed. And sex was on the minds of men and women in equal doses. Husbands and wives were evenly matched in conducting extra-marital affairs. Rubelkov even hacked the emails of his parents. His mom and his dad had already had several torrid excursions, expertly concealed over several years. At first, Rubelkov could not understand their impregnable aplomb and composure, but then he began to acquire it.

To succeed in the world, undetected, was far more challenging than winning a few high-publicity chess games against grandmaster opponents. Yet success and mystery were best exemplified by the tinted windowed caravans transporting unnamed Russian-speaking men surrounded by bodyguards. Rubelkov saw the caravans on his way to his international school in Tillin's downtown area. The Audi and Mercedes SUVs would park outside of a bank or an office building that housed law and accounting firms. Very often, a stunning woman in tight clothes and sunglasses would walk next to a Protected One.

Once, from the window of a bathroom in his school, Rubelkov aimed a pocket sound surveillance scope he had built. He pointed the scope at a caravan of three Mercedes SUVs that were parked across the street. In an instant it seemed, the doors to one of the SUV's flung open. Rubelkov turned off the device and ducked back from the corner of the window. Two men in gray overcoats began motioning toward Rubelkov's direction. Just then, a weather helicopter from a local television station flew overhead. The two men looked up at the helicopter. The one shielding his eyes from the sun motioned to the other to return to the SUV. Rubelkov breathed evenly and returned to his calculus class taught in English. His device needed improvements. He wanted his own caravan, his own female companions.

When he was nineteen, he asked his father for a loan of 50,000 euros. (Though part of the European Union, Estonia would only later adopt the euro. Estonian kroons would be more difficult to exchange for rubles). Rubelkov was moving to Moscow. His father, for the first time, turned him down.

Then Rubelkov said, "Dad, I know."

"Know what?"

Though not philosophically transcendent, their conversation had immediate practical effect. Just before he left for Moscow with his father's €50,000 and his atheist blessing, Rubelkov tacked on an extra 25,000 of the recently issued currency from his mother.

They essentially had the same conversation. But mother-son bonds run deeper. A fifty percent discount for the privilege of birth was just and proper.

8 DAISY YOUNGLUCK

♦

Although born in the port city of Callao, Peru, Daisy Youngluck grew up in Lima. When Daisy was old enough, her mother, Dora, told her that a man from Singapore named Stanley was her father. Dora had met Stanley (the appellative end-product of Jianyu) one day while cleaning the Callao home of Oscar Villanueva. Oscar owned copper mines in southern Peru.

Daisy's origins started one day as Stanley and Oscar talked on the balcony overlooking the port. Stanley's gaze wandered off toward the living room where Dora's fertile curves moved in swift, bouncing strokes. She wore a neat blue uniform hugging her narrow waist.

"I nee help cleeny my place, too. I borrow her?" Stanley said in jagged English.

"I'm sure your hotel's housekeeping could use an extra hand," Oscar chuckled. "It's up to her." Oscar's English was neat and crisp.

Dora normally had no interest in Asian men, but she noticed the shine on his shoes, the crafted gold watch with Roman numerals, the alligator skin wristband, the sharp corners of his starched white shirt, the sparkle of his cuff links. Later that night in Stanley's hotel suite, Dora understood the English word: "shipping."

Dora did not ever learn Stanley's last name, but knew that "Young" was both a Chinese and English surname. And "Luck" often appeared in both languages. To use her own last name, Alvarez, on Daisy's birth certificate, was to admit conclusively that Daisy was born out of wedlock. So "Youngluck" appeared as the surname on Daisy's birth certificate. Dora picked the name "Daisy" because it sounded a*mericano*.

As his fortunes advanced, Oscar reserved his home in Callao for business meetings and moved to Lima. Dora followed with Daisy in tow. Stanley never returned to Peru, and Oscar never mentioned his name.

It seemed clear to Oscar that Daisy was one of Stanley's many territorial markers, a side bet of genetic material on the roulette table of the human propagation. His dealings with Stanley had made Oscar a wealthy man. He used ships from Stanley's company to transport copper to Singapore and the burgeoning Chinese market. Oscar's profit was enough to compensate him for the brief loss of consortium during Dora's pregnancy. Also, even though Oscar still had his attractive wife, he could tide himself over with a variety of companions provided by certain hotels in Lima.

When the little girl grew, Oscar paid for Daisy's education at the local Catholic school in Lima's San Isidrio district. This was purely a matter of convenience for Oscar. Dora had more time for the house and his corporeal desires if Daisy's school was nearby.

Like her mother, Daisy developed a striking feminine form, but with a lighter complexion. Dora transmitted her high cheek bones, plush lips, and marvelous white teeth. Daisy's unusually upright posture had a different explanation. Perhaps it was the mystery of her origins that also nourished Daisy's proud carriage and precocious curiosity. The first sentence she ever uttered was "*¿Por qué?*" – Why?

Early in life, Daisy began making loose associations about status: Itinerant vendors spoke mostly Quechua, the language of indigenous Peruvians. People working for others spoke mostly Spanish. Owners and employers spoke English. Beautiful women lived or worked in large homes. Men were more careful with beautiful women, and more so, if they were openly intelligent and educated.

Daisy also noticed an ever-so-slight doleful expression on her mother's face as she went about her work. The expression bordered on a wince; in fact, a wince is what it was. The wince inverted into a broad smile when Daisy came face to face with her mother, but returned again when Dora looked in another direction. *¿Por qué?* Then Dora once saw Oscar squeeze Dora's rear as she passed him. The wince came on, but Dora said nothing.

When Daisy was twelve, she woke up one morning and felt pain in her chest and nipples. She saw they were swollen and red. She showed them to her mother. Her mother smiled. Weeks, then months, passed with varying degrees of pain and swelling. At thirteen, Daisy had her first period. Then her curves started to fill. In three years, the protrusion atop her long legs was a glorious counterbalance for the buoyant vessels lolling on her chest. Daisy's walk to school became a neighborhood event. At first, there were a few more energetic *¡Buenos días!* from suited men being driven to the office. Then several of the neighborhood's businessmen, erstwhile paragons of taste and decorum of Peruvian society, began offering her complimentary transportation to school, just two blocks away.

With her magnificent carriage, upright yet relaxed, Daisy calmly declined the offers. Yet, when Oscar started looking past her mother, Daisy's traffic-stopping body tightened. Daisy met Oscar's first attempt with an elbow to the wrist of his open hand. *¡A mí, no!* But she knew that Oscar would continue and that one day she would have to relent. Daisy wanted to stay in school long enough to learn English and math. Yet, even if she gave up her body one day, Daisy promised herself, she would never truly submit to a man.

9 KRYSHA

Before 1991, private property in Russia was an official rarity. A decade later, however, Russian billionaires became a standard news item. It did not take long for Sergei Rubelkov to recognize that political roofing from the Kremlin – *krysha* as the Russians called it – was essential. Rubelkov's rise was as meteoric as the rest. He first got wind of the plans for a gas pipeline from the Ukraine after tracking a Mercedes SUV caravan through the streets of Moscow for several weeks.

The first step was getting the signal from a cell phone of one of the security personnel of the entourage. Courtesans – male, female, she-male, transsexual, whatever was in order – were the main sources. If the target liked the encounter, he quickly coughed up his cell phone number. The chemistry had to be right. Identify the sexual preference. Create the nonobvious, uncontrived meet up. Satisfy the desire. The more skilled ones did not ask "Do you like?" They knew by observing and did what worked. Rubelkov compensated these reconnaissance specialists well.

After obtaining a cell number, Rubelkov easily followed the caravan. Most of the negotiations happened at Natinka's, a dance club near Lotte Plaza. With Russian eye candy swirling in the flashing lights, Natinka's was also a hotspot for speed chess over house vodka, Tennessee whiskey and Puerto Rican rum. In a few nights, Rubelkov casually earned a reputation as the club's chess pro. Challengers sat down across from him and, before their minute on the chess clock was up, they slumped away muttering variations of a standard line about having too much to drink.

But Rubelkov had matched them glass-for-glass with Don Q, Ron del Barrilito, Ron Llave or Palo Viejo on the rocks. From time to time, he also drank Bacardí, whose origins are Cuban, provided that the fresh bottle was labeled "Puerto Rican Rum" and he cracked opened the top himself. For Rubelkov, Puerto Rican rum, not vodka, or any other distillation, was the most effective countermeasure for the harsh Russian winter. Such was his respect for Puerto Rican rum that Rubelkov hypothesized that Russian history would have taken distinctly French and then Germanic turns had the invading forces of Napoleon and Hitler been adequately provisioned with the fermented liquid.

Taking a brief moment away to refresh their drinks, two large members of the caravan in tailored wool suits stopped to try their hand. Bobbing his curly black hair, Rubelkov feigned humility as each walked away with a subtle nod of acknowledgment that the chess game was over. As the second one walked away, Rubelkov asked: "Are you with Petrovich?" When Rubelkov received no answer, he knew.

The caravan belonged to Mikhail Petrovich, a pioneer of Russia's private oil and gas industry. His *krysha* with Kremlin regulars, former members of the Politburo and the KGB, was legendary. Petrovich was also a phenomenon with numbers. Nevertheless, the skill to hold in his mind and choose quickly from daunting sequences of moves and countermoves on the checkered board had eluded him.

In a plush velvet booth beyond the flash and rumble of techno music, Petrovich pondered the ways to exploit for himself Russia's need for Ukrainian gas.

Smoothing the sides of his neatly cropped gray beard, Petrovich glanced over at the chess tables on the other end of the club. The two entourage members returned.

"You didn't last very long." Petrovich said to them. "Invite the kid over."

Rubelkov was summoned. Petrovich thought he could use Rubelkov. Rubelkov knew he would use Petrovich. Both were right. Rubelkov shook Petrovich's hand and exerted slightly extra pressure on Petrovich's little finger on which he wore a gold signet ring with a flat black stone. After receiving permission, Rubelkov sat down in the booth. A bodyguard stayed between him a Petrovich.

Petrovich knew better than to play chess against Rubelkov, but they discussed the game. Their conversation started with Russia's impressive chess history. Petrovich lavished most of his praise on 1970s grandmaster Boris Spassky. He was convinced that Spassky only lost to the American Bobby Fischer because the Americans had drugged Spassky with non-lethal doses of polonium-laced tea. However, Petrovich disputed Garry Kasparov's stature in the game. For Petrovich, it was not so much Kasparov's losses to Deep Blue, an IBM computer that Rubelkov regarded as indisputable proof that machines would surpass the human mind in all intellectual and creative endeavors. For Petrovich, Kasparov – a vocal critic of Russian president Vladimir Putin – was just too transparent and democratic to be revered.

Petrovich and Rubelkov then turned to business and geopolitics, which went hand in hand. The breakup of the Soviet Union brought private enterprise, a compelling incentive to work hard for material rewards. The Soviet dispersion left Russia wounded and diminished, its superpower status gone, perhaps, irretrievably. The way forward was confounding. China was not a natural ally. Russia needed China. China did not need Russia – at least not anymore.

To feel patriotism for Russia required an implausible harmonization of its schizoid past – from imperial tsars standing high above peasant masses, to the false, classless ideology of the Politburo, to the Kremlin-sponsored oligarchs who now ran the show from secure high rises in London or New York, or from secret dachas on the shores of the Black Sea, or from heli-padded yachts in the Caribbean. What compelling reasons would justify defending the nation's sprawling arctic forests and tundra, the angry, inconsolable and determined cries that evolved into the Russian language, and the long-suffering Russian character? If the Russian military could not produce material or psychic rewards, who would fight for Russia's elusive identity?

Outside of the Asian continent, Russia's influence had become half-hearted and erratic. Activities in Cuba and Angola were simply too expensive and yielded paltry returns. Hugo Chávez made a few token overtures for Russia to invest in Venezuela. Yet, Chávez was nationalizing industries left and right. There would be no return to a communist economy. World oil prices made Russia's energy industry strong. Still, Russian wages were relatively high, so the country did not receive the torrent of dollars that China was using to buy weapons and rights to minerals and seaports. Now, in early 2008, Rubelkov remarked how quickly China had advanced in negotiations with Pakistan to open a naval base in Gwadar, a Pakistani port city near the Persian Gulf. Members of his *krysha* had told Petrovich about these secret China-Pakistan negotiations. Petrovich was struck that Rubelkov knew this too, but how? Petrovich could use this man.

Petrovich's self-regard insisted that he still had an experiential edge over the much younger Rubelkov. Nevertheless, it was Rubelkov who came up with the Russian threat to invade the Ukraine if the pipeline deal was not done on Russia's terms. Russia still had tanks, soldiers, guns and nuclear arms (although not all of the latter could be readily located or accounted for).

The threat would come from Russia's incursion into the Republic of Georgia. The invasion of Georgia in April 2008 was but a signal that the Ukraine was next. As in chess, and as Rubelkov proposed to Petrovich, who in turn urged the Kremlin, the threat is often more effective than its realization. The Ukraine pipeline deal earned a fortune for Petrovich, Rubelkov and a few select shingles of Petrovich's *krysha*. A short time thereafter, the former prime minister of the Ukraine would go to prison for striking the disastrous, one-sided pipeline deal for her country. But that is another story.

Rubelkov now had enough cash on hand to do another deal – on his own. However, he would have to shake off Petrovich or at least keep him at bay. Although Rubelkov had truly earned his take in the Ukraine pipeline deal, it was Petrovich's mindset that Rubelkov would always remain in his debt. Rubelkov could go wherever he wanted. Petrovich would find him. This just meant that Rubelkov would just have to know when Petrovich was near.

With their initial handshake, Rubelkov had pasted a magnetized sliver of metal onto Petrovich's signet ring. It was smaller than the size of a confetti glitter flake and blended with the gold ring. The impermeable gold flake contained a solar-powered tracking chip. It needed just half an hour of light per day to stay active. As long as Petrovich wore the ring, Rubelkov would know where he was. This was important because Petrovich was known to micromanage the time, place and manner of an execution – *razborka* was the Russian term. After the body was down and bloody, Petrovich would play the innocent onlooker and walk past the victim just to make sure the sniper's headshot was good enough to instantly stop the breathing.

In striking off on his own, Rubelkov also wanted a warmer climate. With his Estonian citizenship, Rubelkov carried a European Union passport. This greatly simplified travel to the U.S. Rubelkov booked a commercial flight to London, then New York and then San Juan. Even in warm weather, Puerto Rican rum would be tasty.

10 DIOSA

As Daisy Youngluck completed high school in Lima, her worldly views departed from the Catholic themes of her formal education. She watched young teacher nuns leave abruptly from the institution. She later saw them in pumps and makeup while they shopped in Lima's upscale malls or drove European sedans with their children in snappy clothes. Most of these women did not even approach Daisy's extraordinary looks. Yet Daisy could not bear the thought of living in one house, waiting for one man to bring her what she wanted. The one man often ended up sharing the fruits of his efforts with several women. In Daisy's eyes, the speculation, uncertainty and the diminishing returns of this arrangement made it a fool's gamble. Better to be a price maker than a price taker.

So she relaxed her guard around Oscar Villanueva. He had now grayed considerably, his belt buckle disappearing under the fold of his belly. She started walking closer to him if they entered the same room of his home. She needed her first clinical encounter, one where she was in total control and knew exactly what she was doing. Her mother had also felt him. *So what?* That's only a mental distraction that Daisy could ignore.

Be soft and yielding. Make him need you, but – most vitally – find out his fears. Learn what makes this man crumble.

Secure and relaxed in the warm tenderness of Daisy's flesh, Oscar opened his vault of business secrets – those expensive lessons otherwise learned only in the fog and fury of commercial warfare. She learned that the serum of sex softens otherwise hard men. A man's command, strength and decisiveness faded in proportion to his growing desire for her until, eventually, the man he once believed himself to be was nothing but a small, lost boy looking helplessly for his mother.

Daisy did not limit herself to one instructor. She discreetly submitted her magnificent body to the touch of the other established men in the neighborhood. And through them, Daisy got sight of the broader world – a world that she needed to see firsthand. The most important pre-departure lesson, the one uniformly and implicitly conveyed by her unwitting teachers, was that it took great courage to steal. Moreover, the larger the amount stolen, the less it looked like theft and the more it enjoyed the aura of a shrewd masterstroke. In this connection, a vital trait of most human beings is that they often forget how much they have and where it is located.

A thoughtful South American businessman usually keeps his money in U.S. dollars. Trips to Miami, New York and Los Angeles are often described as "a vacation" to U.S. immigration inspectors and consular officials. Yet their main purpose is to ensure that there is still ready access to U.S. checking accounts and safety deposit boxes holding untaxed earnings. Daisy made an impressive trophy on these trips, in platform pumps and tight, bright dresses just covering her luscious thighs. An expensive necklace of gold or pearls, given by her companions, could not deflect the eyes drawn to her fabulous chest. In short order, Daisy learned the locations, names, accounts, signatures and passwords of her proud, self-assured patrons.

In two years, when she was twenty-one, Daisy had caressed enough cash to start a business making and distributing cosmetics. She called her business "Diosa," the Spanish word for "Goddess." She learned that by organizing a U.S. corporation and becoming an "intra-company transfer," she could routinely enter the country on her own without having to go as frequently to the U.S. Embassy in Lima for a visa. Her company first rented a small storefront in New York City on Broadway in Greenwich Village.

She then began prospecting for "mentors" from Wall Street and the Upper East Side. Her U.S.-domiciled consorts kept more significant cash sums, in the hundreds of thousands, in their homes and apartments. The largest amounts, however, were virtually inaccessible in foreign accounts in places like Guernsey, the Channel Islands and Mauritius. Stand-in offshore executives, usually foreign-based lawyers, managed the accounts through powers-of-attorney and origamic chains of legal entities so that the true owner's footprints never showed on the trail.

Daisy spoke English fluently, but her Spanish accent surfaced from time to time. It irritated her when someone would ask to repeat herself when she pronounced the word "it" as "eet" or "is" and "eez." In

New York, she noticed animus against Hispanics. During dinner dates, she often observed a sidelong sneer by her tall, white companions as they gave their order to a Latino-looking waiter. These men of expensive education and refinement seemed to forget that she was part Latina. She blunted the sharp edge of this thought, knowing that, by their third date, this cocksure lawyer, investment banker, or overgrown trust-fund brat would hand over a road map to an easy five figures in cash.

She reinvested the "tips" in her cosmetics company.

Diosa lipstick, eyeliner and mascara gathered a following among Latina women in the U.S. – first in New York, then Chicago, Miami, and finally in Los Angeles. To stoke their mystique, Diosa labels claimed that ingredients were "sourced from remote villages in the Amazon jungle." For the environmentally conscious, the packaging was purportedly made from recycled materials. Diosa's U.S. advertising slogan was "*Pick your men.*" Consultants tried to persuade Daisy to use the singular "*Pick your man,*" but Daisy brushed aside their concerns.

When several red carpet celebrities started using the brand, Diosa caught fire. In six or seven years, Daisy did not need men at all. Distribution expanded throughout the U.S. The company created more than 10,000 jobs and qualified Daisy for U.S. permanent resident status and then citizenship. There were Diosa reps in almost every major U.S. city and town. Only in her early 30s, $10 million a month was pouring in, and Daisy wanted to diversify her holdings. While her company's financial statements were entirely private, Daisy received unsolicited ten-digit offers from multinational cosmetics companies.

One icy Friday evening, after rejecting another buyout offer, Daisy wanted relief from the New York cold. She kept a carry-on bag in her office with a couple of days' worth of clothes. She could buy a bathing suit later. This would be just for the weekend. So Peru was too far. Besides, any place outside of the U.S. required a passport, which Daisy had left at home, in her sprawling uptown condo. Lack of a passport also ruled out Jamaica and the Dominican Republic. Daisy consulted a map and the weather reports. Miami was amazingly cold with the temperatures dipping into the 50s. Daisy vaguely remembered this, but felt slightly embarrassed in confirming with one of her executives, that no visa or a passport was needed to travel to Puerto Rico. A New York driver's license sufficed as identification.

Daisy summoned Rob Swisher. Rob was thick-necked, burly, and gay. Rob had had a brief career as a linebacker in the National Football League. None of his fellow players ever found out, but it became too taxing for Rob to control his pelvic excitement in the locker room. He had played in two Pro Bowls, and one-on-one, he was feared by players. But the unspoken rule in the NFL was that players who "came out" got hurt, even by their own teammates. So he quit gracefully. After football, Rob sought jobs as a personal security escort. He landed an interview with Daisy by extolling Diosa's eyeliner in the first sentence of his cover letter. Daisy hired him on the condition that he *"never, ever, ever"* wear makeup in her presence.

Four and a half hours after takeoff, Daisy and Rob arrived at Luis Muñoz Marín airport in San Juan. A five-minute taxi ride and they were at The Ritz-Carlton hotel in Isla Verde. They had adjoining rooms with Daisy sleeping in the larger one. In public, at the right times, Daisy and Rob held hands for cover. With Rob posing as her companion, Daisy spent the first few days dozing on the beach, reading Richard Dawkins' *The Selfish Gene*, while Rob sipped nonalcoholic *piña coladas*. She ordered food in her own language. Despite Rob's presence, an occasional male passerby ogled at her riveting, bronzed physique laid out on a hotel lounge chair. Used to the male attention during her Peruvian school days, Daisy felt comfortable. The thought of returning to New York produced a slight dread. She wanted to stay.

She and Rob hired a town car for the day. They drove down Ashford Avenue in Condado and stopped at La Ventana Al Mar, the open beachside park. Daisy stepped out of the car in the brilliant sun. The breeze swept back her brown, flowing hair as she walked across the open grass toward the oceanside walkway. Knowing that the majestic view of the ocean would always be open here, Daisy turned around and spotted a fifteen-story building, The Girasol, across Ashford.

The next day, she hired a local lawyer who identified the owners of the top two floors. She paid $5 million in cash. She built a spiral staircase and installed a personal elevator connecting the two floors.

Within a few months, Daisy sold Diosa to Jeune Poisson, S.A. a French conglomerate. With a little more than $3 billion, Daisy was, for a brief period, the wealthiest resident of Puerto Rico. Without her company to run, however, she became restless. She sampled all of Puerto Rico's major hotels and resorts. She was taken aback by how little effort was devoted to impressing guests. Frequently, the sidewalks and approaches to the hotels had trash and cigarette butts. Even the sand behind the beachfront hotels sometimes had litter or broken glass.

Why doesn't management, as a standard practice, have employees clean this up? Send someone out every fifteen minutes. It makes no difference that the trash is beyond hotel property. Everything in the vicinity must be spotless – Daisy thought to herself.

Valet men, reception personnel, waitresses, bartenders often failed to greet visitors with a friendly face and salutation. *Doesn't anyone train them?*

Daisy wanted her own hotel.

11 POCKET CHANGE

♦

During the 1990s, Wen Kashing continued as a dealer in Macau and moved up in casino size. About thirty-seven miles southwest of Hong Kong, Macau had been a Portuguese territory until 1999 when it became a special administrative region of China. Macau consists of the Macau peninsula connected to two islands, Taipa and Coloane. Most of its half million residents live on the peninsula comprising less than nine square miles. The Cotai resort district was later created between the two islands by landfill of about four and a half square miles. The government's main sources of revenue are gaming and tourism.

Wen worked his way up from the Casa Real to the Lisboa and then the Altira. He became well-known among dealers, croupiers, and pit bosses. He learned the business and the limitless ways to take a player's money. He also continued his payday loans. His fellow dealers and croupiers were good credit risks because they got tipped every day. Wen would approach a late payer with a smile, leaning back, shoulders relaxed. Wen knew that parting with tips was less painful than handing over a portion of one's paycheck. There was also Wen's threatening, confident manner. His customers paid because they wanted to pay. He kept accounts in his head. He did not display anal, bean-counting tendencies that got one killed in Macau. Privately, however, Wen double-checked the balances on a laptop back inside his spanked-out condo in the Royal Arc residential zone.

In mornings before work, Wen reviewed his loan portfolio outside on his condo's twentieth floor balcony. He smoked a Boriqua Puro Puerto Rican cigar. He had been smoking these for years. Toasty and complex, they helped him concentrate. At any given time, Wen maintained a three-month stock of Boriqua Puros in a humidor. He had learned about these handmade smokes from a Swiss blackjack player at the Altira. Instead of a tip, the player gave him a Boriqua Puro.

The player said in a German accent: "Forget about the Cubans. It gets cold there. The tobacco leaves don't grow the right way." Upon arriving home that morning, Wen looked up Puerto Rico on the Internet. The island lay further south from Cuba, more distant, easterly, in the Gulf Stream.

Intriguing. One day, I'll pay a visit.

Wen's lending business usually ran without a hitch. Those borrowers who paid could borrow again. Those who caused trouble, however, suffered a permanent corporal etching, usually a deep slash on the thigh or shoulder. A healthy supply of Macanese street thugs and fixers allowed Wen to drive down his "recovery" costs. With sunglasses, hats, headbands and long coats, Wen's contractors were difficult to tell apart or trace. After a collections call, they vanished in the streets like storm water flowing into drains. With crime thriving in Macau, deniability was always plausible. After a deadbeat had been "branded," Wen extended no further credit.

Wen would gesture toward his former customer's thigh or shoulder: "I understand my honorable friend's circumstances, but your earnings prospects have diminished, have they not?" Most dealers and croupiers understood English.

On occasion, recalcitrant borrowers were never seen again. The first involved a loan to a baccarat dealer at the Grand Lisboa for 400,000 patacas, just under $50,000. The dealer began avoiding Wen and then disputed the balance. Wen visited the Three Lamps garment district. He interviewed a contractor who wanted ten percent of the unpaid balance as a "recovery" fee. (There would be no actual recovery of money owed; the client was simply going to die). Wen leaned back and smiled. They agreed to five percent. At first, Wen was a little uneasy. But after the first hit, Wen did not hesitate the next time. It did wonders for his "loan realization rate." At that time, the knifings and the killings were unlikely to come back to him. Macau investigators and prosecutors knew that convictions were difficult since execution-style murders in Macau were commonplace in the 1990s. Finally and perhaps most importantly, collection calls by his Macanese contractors worked faster and were less expensive than hiring a lawyer.

Maiming and death, however, were not Wen's goals. His objective was to make enough money to buy a resort and gaming license. Having your loans honored required credibility, and credibility required the ability to inflict harm. Wen used his credit management skills to start a chain of storefront payday loan shops, known as Caixa Kashing. At ten percent interest per week, these loans of no more than 1,000 patacas (about $125) paid off handsomely. The financial innovation of which Wen was quite proud, given the maximum sum involved, was taking possession of the customer's working cell phone, replete with passwords and stored information, as collateral for the loan. In five years, still in his early 30s, Wen had more than 50 locations in Macau. Caixa Kashing expanded into Hong Kong and opened more than 100 locations. His mother Jia never found out these were his. Plausible deniability. Caixa Kashing evolved into a full-scale bank with an emphasis on that chimerical activity of "private banking." A considerable profit center became helping mainland Chinese visitors evade the government's 20,000 Yuan limit (about $3,175) on cash transfers into Macau. To undermine this ignoble restraint of trade, Caixa Kashing employed a variety of fake import-export transactions and debit card schemes.

In 2002, as Wen approached 40, he and Lee Fook were mentioned in the same paragraphs of the *South China Morning Post* as two of Asia's wealthiest men. Fook's estimated wealth was $5 billion. Wen assiduously denied all appraisals of his own comparable wealth. At about this time, Macau ended its government monopoly of the gaming industry and started granting concessions to private parties. Wynn Resorts, Las Vegas Sands and MGM-Mirage were awarded concessions. Partnering with Fook, other casino and hotel operators secured concessions. By 2007, Macau's gambling revenue surpassed that of Las Vegas.

Wen proposed a $1.5 billion, 2,000-room hotel and casino next to the Las Vegas Sands' larger replica of the Venetian in the Cotai district. Instead, Macau's gaming commission offered him only a subconcession to operate the table games at Macau's Emperor King. Space for 200,000 square feet of table games was nothing to sneeze at. Without Fook's patronage, Wen was fortunate to be offered the subconcession. Yet Wen wanted a full-service property, including a hotel. He envisioned living in the penthouse of his own hotel to be named The Magellan. He planned to lean back with his relaxed shoulders and strut down the carpeted gaming floors while smoking a Boriqua Puro. He wanted to "comp" high rollers himself. He wanted total honesty-inducing command over his dealers, croupiers and pit bosses. There would be random quality control visits to the baccarat and blackjack tables, the hotel restaurants, the performance arenas and theaters.

Yet, help from Fook would never happen. Or it would be obscenely expensive. Fook had lorded over

Macau's gaming industry for too long. This was a good business. But, remarkably, Wen was simply too late to the real game in Macau. He wanted to be in the business, but where? Regulation of Caixa Kashing was increasing, and rumors about Wen's underworld tactics had grown over the years. As Macau's gaming industry started to soar, police became more diligent at reducing violent crime. It was time for a transition. Wen had still not paid the $250 million subconcession fee. Again, where could he go? Sean Wyman, Sherman Abelman, and Ken Kicklighter were too dominant in Las Vegas. Atlantic City had matured and was too far north. Cy Kilmer had locks on South Africa and the Bahamas. The Dominican Republic was overbuilt.

One cool Macau evening, Wen sat on the balcony of a new penthouse condo. He slowly drew smoke from a Boriqua Puro cigar as he looked toward the white glow of the 1,000-foot Macau Tower and the Sai Van Bridge. In a pale yellow handmade guayabera and beige khaki pants, Wen sat down and propped up his long legs and black suede Belgian loafers on the guardrail. He opened his laptop to place an order for a fresh batch of Puerto Rican cigars. With idle curiosity, he typed in "Puerto Rico" in a general search. On the third link down, Wen saw a report that the U.S. Navy was auctioning off parts of thirteen-square-mile property on the east coast of the island. Roosevelt Roads.

Thirteen square miles? About the combined size of the Macau peninsula and Cotai. And Macau was cold in winter — Wen thought.

The minimum bid for the first 2,900 acres, more than four and a half square miles – as big as Cotai— was $65 million.

Pocket change. I'll offer $50 million.

12 THE VALUE OF REAL

♦

On a plane back from San Juan, Lino Mendoza opened his computer and started a spreadsheet of observations. The foundations of Puerto Rico City emerged. Several cities served as reference points, but Las Vegas, Atlantic City and Macau were the main baselines.

Before Atlantic City opened for gambling in 1978, Puerto Rico and Nevada were the only two U.S. jurisdictions where gambling was legal. There were historic traces of honest efforts to put Puerto Rico on the map as a premiere gaming and entertainment destination. Many photographs in John Scarne's 1961 classic *The Complete Guide to Gambling* were taken in the El San Juan and Caribe Hilton casinos. In the 1960s, Nat King Cole, Eddie Fisher, and Sammy Davis Jr. performed at the El San Juan's Tropicoro, accommodating perhaps just two hundred people. Instead of building upon these beginnings as done in Las Vegas, Puerto Rico relegated tourism to secondary status. The island policy makers focused on replacing sugarcane, coffee, pineapple and tobacco fields with cement houses and tax-exempt manufacturing facilities. Manufacturing was impressive and dignifying. Tourism unavoidably amounted to low paying, menial jobs. Or so they thought.

By ending the federal tax breaks, the U.S. Congress exposed Puerto Rico's manufacturing for the fallacy that it was. The former sugarcane fields in the coastal plains, where many of the pharmaceutical plants had been built, started turning into noxious heaps of abandoned cement buildings, rusting pipes and empty pressure vessels. Local policy makers could not seem to understand that the world's most precious asset would be an environment of attraction and enjoyment sheltered from the din and dirt of global Industrialization.

Surrounded by desert, Las Vegas was bounded on the west by U.S. Interstate 15 – a clogged aorta of metal and fumes at least twice a day. The prime segment of the Las Vegas Strip, from The Wynn to the MGM Grand, was less than two miles long. South Las Vegas Boulevard carried two-way traffic through the Strip. Pedestrians inhaled exhaust from cars, taxis, and tour buses. They either took elevated walkways to cross the boulevard or waited for the traffic lights to change while staying wary of aggressive and drunk drivers.

Lino looked at the satellite photograph of Roosevelt Roads saved on his computer. Puerto Rico City would have more than three miles of waterfront arching around the horseshoe-shaped harbor. Its own pedestrian-friendly array of hotels, restaurants, and clubs would be wedged between the ocean and the lush tropical mountains. There was easily enough space for ten to fifteen hotels, adding 30,000 new hotel rooms, more than double the existing and paltry 13,000-room inventory of the entire Puerto Rican archipelago. The Puerto Rico City airport would be set back further inland but still only about a mile from the closest point of the harbor. A truly walkable city, uncluttered by automotive transportation was completely possible. Each building and structure would be situated strategically to protect the mangroves, the coconut trees, and the shoreline.

Still, the Las Vegas Strip was diversified with the full spectrum of choices, tastes and price points. Don't want to pay $60 dollars for a bottle of California sparkling at the Bellagio? Walk across the street and buy it for $15 at a liquor store. Better yet – you can carry the bottle back to your room in plain view of the Bellagio hotel staff. Wander into Caesar's Palace or The Venetian at night with shorts and sandals just to look around? No problem. Trying this at a hotel in Puerto Rico risked public embarrassment.

Puerto Rico mostly catered to the exclusive, upscale traveler. The visitor was often held captive inside of a compound resort. Then, he or she was ruthlessly and systematically nicked by stratospheric pricing. Someone walking into a hotel to play at the casino or have dinner could be accosted by staff with insulting or suspicious demeanor to confirm his or her business. Such embarrassments were a rare occurrence in Las Vegas or Atlantic City. The local Puerto Rican visitor was often, although not the exclusive, object of this indignity. Puerto Rican service could be surly and defiant. It was a running joke that certain bars of San Juan's major hotels were the only ones certified by

Alcoholics Anonymous, because getting a drink was nearly impossible. New rules sprung up almost without warning. A smoking ban? Atlantic City started one too, and a good number of visitors who liked to smoke stopped coming.

Puerto Rico City would have to be different. Nothing ruins a vacation more than being neglected or ignored, or bossed around by petty rules. People want their drinks now and with a smile. Let them light up and relax. Let them walk outside with cocktails in biodegradable cups and sunbathe au naturale like Europeans – Lino though to himself.

In 2007, after a bidding war in Las Vegas, a closely held real estate firm paid about $30 million per acre for the 34 acres sitting under the outdated Tropicana Hotel & Casino. The buyer planned to demolish the building and invest an additional $2 billion in 9,000 new rooms. In another deal, an Australian gambling company planned to pay $475 million for a 27-acre site. This came to $17.6 million an acre. In yet another Las Vegas deal, an Israeli group paid $34 million an acre for the New Frontier hotel, which was later imploded. The MGM-Mirage was going to spend $8 billion to construct CityCenter with 5,000 rooms on 76 acres in between the Monte Carlo and the Bellagio. Over a period of about five years, projects involving 45,000 new hotel rooms worth $35 billion were planned for the Las Vegas Strip alone.

Meanwhile, Puerto Rico's largest hotel was El Conquistador with just 984 rooms.

Half a world away, in Macau, the Las Vegas Sands Corporation spent $2.2 billion on a larger replica of the Venetian with 3,000 rooms. The company planned to invest an additional $13 billion to create a diversified entertainment district in Cotai, a former marshland in Taipa across a set of causeways. A new airline, Viva Macau, would fly in high rollers from Indonesia.

Puerto Rico Air should have happened long ago. If Jamaica and the Dominican Republic could have their own dedicated airlines, Puerto Rico Air followed perforce.

In another part of Asia, Songdo rose up in the gray skies of South Korea. Gale International, a Boston-based developer, created the master plan for the spanking-new 1,500-acre city. The South Korean government would invest $10 billion just in infrastructure. A seven-mile bridge would connect Songdo to the Incheon International Airport. Seoul, the capital of South Korea, would be a 35-mile subway ride away.

A seven-mile bridge could connect Vieques to Puerto Rico City. A rail system from Puerto Rico City to San Juan would also be about 35 miles long – Lino thought to himself.

In the Middle East, billions of dollars were pouring into Dubai's waterfront, including the creation of artificial islands with vacation mansions offshore in Persian Gulf. Dubai was planning the Burj Khalifa, the world's tallest building.

Puerto Rico City could not be merely a "resort town." It must be a city on the scale of Las Vegas, Dubai and Macau. It must include the careful planning of a Songdo. The investment must be in the tens of billions.

Macau and Dubai were not true threats. They could never turn into weekend getaways for the American traveler, especially from the East Coast. As for Las Vegas, you could take your bathing suit, but only hope for warm weather during the fall and winter. Still worse, snow in Las Vegas, even as late as March, was not out of the question. This modular adult park was built entirely in a desert wasteland and was close enough to a 1950s nuclear test site for tourists to have seen the mushroom clouds. Hence, the former naval bombing practice in nearby Vieques and Culebra would also become a historical novelty for Puerto Rico City. This unsettling history would perish into a background of white sands, turquoise water and tropical flora. Beyond Vieques and Culebra were the Virgin Islands. Las Vegas and Atlantic City could not compete with the chance to dock one's boat in the Puerto Rico City harbor, party it up a few days, and then sail off with your A-list friends for a few days in St. Thomas, St. John and St. Croix.

Then there was also the distance to Puerto Rico from the U.S. mainland over water. Yes, Los Angeles and Las Vegas were only four and half hours apart by car, but at least 35 million visitors, including Lino, arrived by plane each year. Hawaii, which was a thousand miles farther from the mainland, airlifted enough visitors to justify having 32,000 more hotel rooms than Puerto Rico.

Puerto Rico Air. Puerto Rico Air.

Yet, what about Puerto Rico's reputation for crime? Las Vegas had been controlled by the mafia. Macau had been infested with gangs and street killings. One could also root out most violent crime by getting rid of its primary motivation: Drug profits. A fully conscious adult has the inalienable right to poison himself. A grown man or woman wants to drink sulfuric acid , gasoline, or 2,000 calories of sugar drinks per day? That's their business. Decriminalize drugs.

And the Dominican Republic and post-embargo Cuba? As long as Puerto Rico remained a U.S. territory, these sister, but foreign, islands were not serious threats. The overwhelming majority of Americans do not want to hassle with a passport or visa before they travel. Sixty to seventy percent of Americans don't even have a passport. And who wants to be searched in customs? Lino remembered the time that Dominican Republic customs officials confiscated his pair of green slacks "because they looked like military attire." Puerto Rico was a domestic flight to and from the U.S. Forget about a passport. Forget customs. Buy same-day tickets, bring a picture ID, and you're good to go. Upon arrival, walk straight out of the airplane and get your ride.

Also, winter morning temperatures in Havana are in the 40s. Lying further north, Miami and the Bahamas suffer the same cold snaps. Given Puerto Rico City's year-round warm temperature, outdoor and aquatic activities would deemphasize gambling.

For Lino, the matter was simple: Puerto Rico was grossly underdeveloped to compete at what it could do best.

Yet Lino kept returning to the basic questions: how much was the land worth and who could buy it?

Microsoft had just offered $46 billion for Yahoo!, a website.

A website!

Anyone with access to the Internet and a couple of hundred dollars could get their own. Every nanosecond, a new website was born. But who could create thirteen-square miles of tropical oceanfront land that was part of the United States and reachable by air in less than four hours from the East Coast?

13 NO SECOND CHANCE

♦

In New York, Lino dug into the details of the planned sale of Roosevelt Roads. In broad strokes, the U.S. Navy was going to auction off the federal land to private buyers. The buyers would then have to conform to the Puerto Rico government's reuse plan. Lino grimaced and shook his head. The local government reuse plan carved up the property into a hodgepodge of economic development fantasies and political handouts. A science park for high-tech industries? Another university campus? Residential homes, including low-income housing? Then, and only as an afterthought, the Puerto Rico government "recognizes the need for the development of *moderate* tourism in Puerto Rico," the reuse plan stated.

Moderate?

A few months would decide the destiny of the thirteen-square-mile landmass – the last contiguous piece of oceanfront Puerto Rican land large enough to be shaped and designed into something lasting and important. Already with two airport runways, it was larger than the Macau peninsula and Monaco combined.

By historical irony, the newly available land had been preserved by the American invaders to rescue Puerto Rico from itself. For Lino, only the two runways of the airport should be kept. Almost every other structure, including the military housing and schools, had to be demolished. A new city, planned to the last centimeter, must be built, a city that would replace San Juan as the new epicenter. This could not be another Isla Verde, a district next to the Muñoz Marín airport in San Juan. Family condos, some faded and in disrepair, detracted from Isla Verde's impressive shoreline. Residential property did not produce lasting employment.

Most crucially, Puerto Rico City could not be another exclusive, single owner resort, such as El Conquistador, Palmas Del Mar or Río Mar, surrounded by expensive villas and beach homes. The local populace would resent another enclave from which they were excluded. The enclave model kept the resorts static, complacent and, ultimately, boring.

Puerto Rico City must be diverse and dynamic, containing a complete spectrum of choices: Build the Don Q Castle Hotel where a suite will go for $3,000 a night. But have rooms at the Bohío Guest House for $30. Offer music from opera to reggaeton. Cognac to tropical rum moonshine. Expensive cigars to cheap roll-your-owns with a kick. Under no circumstances should there be residential homes. The mystique and the enticement of Puerto Rico City are that a visit is always temporary. The city needs solar and wind power, hurricane-resistant hotels and casinos, sleek rail transportation, a pedestrian promenade with no cars in sight, marquee lights for shows and world championship sporting events.

Puerto Ricans would finally parlay their expertise in arts, entertainment and sports to create the place where everyone ultimately wants to be and be seen. The island will find itself and its identity. El Morro and

San Cristóbal forts, El Yunque rainforest, Camuy caverns, the Arecibo radio telescope, the Cabo Rojo cliffs, the bioluminescent bays in La Parguera and Vieques were all fascinating but still, in most travelers' minds, they suffered dilution as scattered points of interest. The critical mass, the international brand, the beacon of meaning will be Puerto Rico City. The world would know instantly what the rest of the island was about, where it was, and how to get there.

The essence would be the pleasure principle, pure and simple. You came to Puerto Rico City for one reason and one reason only: to have a good time. It would be safe, clean and, above all, cool. Undeniably cool. Puerto Rico City would make no other associations. This would lead to a complete redirection of the island's economy. The island would claw back the concrete sprawl and reclaim its natural habitats. Guests would consume homegrown coffee, mangoes, tangerines, bananas, pineapples, sugarcane and tobacco. If there was manufacturing, it would be purpose-driven: Puerto Rican bikinis, sunglasses, surfboards, watercraft, and scuba gear.

Politicians were wrong and should be ignored. The island was not going to refurbish abandoned pharmaceutical plants to become an offshore powerhouse in biotechnology. Puerto Rico was not going to pirate away software programmers from Silicon Valley. Scientists from MIT and Stanford would never resign their tenured positions to come teach and do research at the local universities. This was simply never going to happen. They would, however, come to Puerto Rico City to enjoy themselves and spend their wealth.

Lino digressed: And U.S. statehood? This was an impossibility. There would never be a clear majority in favor of statehood. Puerto Ricans were simply too proud. They wanted to feel that Puerto Rico was their own country. Puerto Rico was the Republic of Texas on jet-fuel testosterone and psychedelic estrogen. No prospect or promise of extra U.S. government benefits would cause the deep Puerto Rican core to sell out. Separately, the U.S. would never accept a Spanish-speaking state. English-speaking Americans migrating to Puerto Rico would demand a local court system and legislature in English. The tension would be intolerable. Then another angle altogether: Without any voting power in the U.S., Puerto Rico could eventually be on its own. The days of easy subsidies were over. The island needed to compete in the world markets without artificial life support.

On many fronts, the Puerto Rican people had been misled. Perhaps the greatest deception was in deflecting them away from their strengths. Providing pleasure and enjoyment to others *and* charging a fair price for these were not shameful activities. They should be embraced as life's highest calling.

The dilemma was stark and clear, and time was running out. The bidding would start in a matter of months. It had already been more than a hundred years since the U.S. had taken Puerto Rico from Spain in 1898. Lino did not need to reflect on the final warning of *One Hundred Years of Solitude* to know that there would be no second chance.

14 THE TOP-UP

♦

Aaron Getz had built a Brooklyn-based stock brokerage firm, Haifa Partners, into a bicoastal investment company. Haifa Partners was scrappy and up-close in its tactics but international in its reach. The firm's West Coast office was in Oakland, California where rent was a bargain. Despite Haifa Partners' name, Getz was its only shareholder. He adopted this name to accentuate a Jewish heritage that he knew almost nothing about, but in which he saw many advantages. The firm's name mitigated the surprise and consternation of his Jewish employees when Getz forgot to acknowledge their families' mitzvahs, sedars, and brises.

Through his company, Getz took temporary positions in a smattering of unrelated firms. Haifa Partners had, directly or indirectly, agitated boards of directors in high-tech companies, media firms, food and beverage producers, clothing retailers, energy companies, and airlines, to name a few. Some target companies were publicly traded. Others were privately owned and had quietly looked for a "cash infusion in order to get to the next level."

Getz preferred private company targets. Acquiring meaningful stakes in publicly traded companies implied all manner of formalities and nuisances: teams of lawyers, public relations firms, and filings under oath with the Securities and Exchange Commissions and other regulators. Legal fees became astronomical. Public relations campaigns trumped financial analysis. Reputation management, both his and of his targets' executives, often became the crux of the endeavor. In this regard, Getz discovered how vital it was to have his name appear prominently in major charities and fund raisers. The primary reason that he and other creatures of the same cut gave to charity was to display the very qualities that they lacked, qualities that would ensure and make permanent only modest financial attainments in life. High-profile charitable giving burnished the illusion of a man motivated by principle, generosity, and concern for humanity. The international travel for "charitable and educational purposes" to exotic and remote places with below average literacy rates accrued tax benefits as well.

Despite the complications and greater costs, Getz's first big scores involved public companies. He would acquire upwards of five percent of the outstanding voting shares, make the necessary regulatory filings announcing his intentions as an investor, then begin a stream of media releases about how overpaid and ineffective the management of the target company had been, how the board members had utterly failed to discharge their fiduciary duties to the shareholders, and how he would maximize shareholder value. Except for the latter, there was a modicum of truth to most of these claims.

Indeed, Getz never sought to vindicate the rights of shareholders as a class. It was *his* shareholdings that needed vindication. This noble achievement followed after publicly shaming and maligning management about its "obscene" compensation. Getz would then finance a proxy battle for votes at shareholders' meetings, combining direct mailings and newspaper advertisements and magazines seeking to install his company's slate of director nominees. In the name of "oppressed and disenfranchised hard-working Mom & Pop investors," Getz condemned the poison pills and staggered boards that "entrenched" management of the target company. With impeccable timing, newspapers, magazines, television networks and Internet news sites received anonymous and ready-for-publication reports about private jet abuse, conflict-of-interest transactions, illegal board investigations, illicit sexual liaisons of top executives and board members. Getz seemed to have a live feed to this data, no matter how obscure or personal.

Meanwhile, Getz would fly to strategy and shareholder meetings using one of his own jets. Getz saw no contradiction, since his company was, indeed, private. He also used his own jets for pleasure. When he was working in New York, a wintertime favorite was Puerto Rico. He started by spending a Christmas and New Years at the El San Juan Hotel in Isla Verde. Sizeable gatherings of attractive Jewish women stayed there during the Christian holidays. But when Getz responded that his mother was Irish Catholic, many turned away, promptly excused themselves or started conversations with other men. He later opted for a more secular environment at La Concha Hotel in Condado. For many other reasons, even with religion off the table, there were still no dice. So to improve his chances, each time before he left New York, Getz invited a different woman to spend seven to ten agonizing days with him.

His approach was abrupt, awkward but impressively direct and persistent. His targets included beauty consultants behind cosmetics counters, hostesses at restaurants, female bartenders, and receptionists at offices other than his own. (He learned an expensive lesson just for asking one of his female employees. The severance/settlement was large enough to maintain her customary lifestyle for two years).

After the abrupt invitation, the women were usually speechless and embarrassed. Then he would reach into an ill-fitting jacket and pull up the pictures of his Dassault Falcon and Gulfstream jets on an iPhone. Yet, almost without exception, those women who packed a bag and left with him the next day did not endure the entire trip with Getz. They found various ways to avoid him – private sun tanning or the women's section of the hotel spa. Or they simply left early without warning.

When Getz wasn't staring at their breasts or legs, he was talking incessantly on the phone while saliva accumulated in the corners of his mouth. The time that Getz spent on the phone was a relief for his hasty companions. He laughed at his own jokes and tried to poke fun at his guests before he got to know them. He asked too many questions. The women suffered blunt queries about their private anatomy. "Are you shaved?" was one of Getz's regular ones.

Getz would touch their arms and legs with his pointy and damp fingers. He left behind cold, moist fingerprints that the women wanted to rub off immediately. A rare smile with his mealy mouth showed tiny crooked chopping bits with a greenish patina. If his dates completely refused (amazingly, some did indulge him a few times), he just ordered out.

While working on a takeover at Ashton & Cavendish, Lino Mendoza had once helped craft a "work around" for a problem involving Getz. Getz had acquired a hair more than ten percent of World Package Services, an international delivery company. Lino's client planned a tender offer to buy 100 percent of the company and absorb it completely by merger. With more than ten percent of the shares, Getz could prevent a back-end, short-form merger and create the delay needed for an additional shareholder meeting. Delay would allow Getz to create all kinds of problems.

Before the takeover device had been widely used in Wall Street M&A, Lino wrote a "top-up" provision in the merger agreement. The "top-up" garnered Lino's client enough newly issued shares to surpass 90 percent and dilute Getz to just under ten percent. Getz filed suit anyway, seeking to block the merger. Getz found out through litigation discovery that it was Lino who had worked the "top-up" into the merger agreement. Getz knew he would lose the case, but he wanted the mandatory early mediation conference so he could see Lino in person. After the mediation, the court dismissed Getz's lawsuit to block the merger. Lino made partner at Ashton & Cavendish the next year.

Despite losing the case, Getz still received a small premium for his World Package shares. This softened the blow somewhat, but the sting lingered underneath Getz's hide. Permanent vengeance against this Puerto Rican attorney, who was twenty years his junior, was a near certainty. Whenever Getz traveled to Puerto Rico, he remembered the "top-up."

15 THE BIDDERS

♦

Lino was not alone in thinking that the $65 million minimum bid for the first 2,900 acres of Roosevelt Roads was almost trivial. Daisy Youngluck, Reed Savage, Wen Kashing and Sergei Rubelkov had quickly and independently reached the same conclusion. Lino's appraisal was based on the magnitude of the recent investments in Las Vegas, Macau and Dubai. Of course, one had to factor in the dampening effect of the Puerto Rico government's reuse plan. There was also Puerto Rico's reputation of being a business quagmire, paralyzed by government inertia, impenetrable regulations, and rigid labor laws that made even justified firings prohibitively costly to employers. Even then, the minimum bid was unrealistically low.

Potential buyers from around the world plucked news about the auction from cyberspace and then sent human probes onto the ground. The officially secret bidder registry filled up with front-company names. Apache Holdings, owned by Reed Savage, was one. Magellan Hospitality, a company controlled by Wen Kashing was another. Sergei Rubelkov would do his bidding through Duma Digikov. Daisy Youngluck, eager for a sprawling hotel resort in a Spanish-speaking part of America, expressed her interest through Makeover Enterprises. Each one wanted the entire 2,900 acres as well as the rest of the base when it was put up for bid. With little effort, each could satisfy the minimum $65 million bid.

As for the Puerto Rico reuse plan, this could be renegotiated after the purchase. Each of the potential buyers had enough cash to sit on the property until they got their way. Savage, Youngluck and Wen essentially had the same idea: They would build a single-owner hotel and casino resort and sell the remainder of the property for upscale housing. The reason for this was simple: Why allow competition nearby? Rubelkov wanted a part-time Caribbean vacation compound of 300 acres. He was then going to expand on his father's footsteps by using the rest of the land as a transshipment port for boats coming to and from the Panama Canal.

Lino knew, however, that for Puerto Rico City to happen, the land comprising the base had to function as one integrated whole. Selling the base off in separate pieces for disparate uses would defeat the essence of Puerto Rico City. Alternatively, allowing the property to come into the hands of a single private owner would remove the crucible of competitive forces needed for an entertainment city that continuously reinvented itself. Separately, industrial use, such as a transshipment depot, would threaten further ecological and aesthetic damage to the island.

Lino had done well as a partner of Ashton & Cavendish, but he did not have anything close to $65 million for the minimum bid. If he sold his New York apartment he could survive for another three years in relative comfort. He needed time to find money, using what he thought were his vast, deep and loyal contacts in the capital markets.

Lino asked for a two-year unpaid sabbatical from Ashton & Cavendish, but the management committee turned him down. In becoming a partner at a major New York law firm, one learns to ask only once for a real favor like this. After a certain stage of a career at Ashton & Cavendish, the most valuable compensation was being able to get extended personal time off without losing one's partnership.

Burton Fletcher, the firm's managing partner, delivered the news. "So what exactly was it that you were going to do? Spend a couple of years in Vegas with a few girls?"

Despite Lino's best efforts, word about his extracurricular activities had leaked out.

Fletcher was pencil-necked and angular. A gold tie pin cut across the knot of an orange and black-striped tie, just to remind you that he had written an undergraduate thesis on an obscure philosophical topic at Princeton. Visibly above his head on the bookcase behind him, Fletcher kept a copy of Laurence Tribe's *American Constitutional Law* to signal his Harvard Law School pedigree. It was an unspoken rule that Harvard graduates did not display their diplomas. A mane of light brown hair swept across the forehead of his narrow face. For $100, he had the sides feathered and layered into trial lawyer's coiffure. Fletcher had never in his career tried a case to a jury. He also kept a picture of his Andover football days behind him on his desk. Yet there was one detail that Lino noticed. The scoreboard in the background showed less than a minute remaining in the fourth quarter, and the score was hopelessly lopsided. In other words, Fletcher had come onto the field once the outcome of the game had been decided – just like now. Fletcher's tiny blue eyes twinkled with delight through horn-rimmed, tortoise shell glass frames.

"Lino you have come a long way. You should be proud, señor."

Señor?

For 14 years, Lino had delivered precisely on time and saved too many silver-spooned asses from their own pomposity in M&A chess matches. But there had always been the "but." Until Lino, this law firm with more than 900 lawyers had never had a Hispanic partner. In addition, black (one) and women (four) partners could be counted exactly on one hand. Moreover, it took Lino eight years, instead of the customary six, to make partner. The urge to fire his legendary snot cannon pulsed in Lino's throat. But the costs would be enormous. Strictly speaking, in most jurisdictions, it would be assault and battery. A criminal conviction, with no lasting material reward, made no sense. Also, Lino had read John O'Hara's *Appointment in Samara*. He was not going to embark on a slow voyage to final doom by throwing a drink in the face of a skinny version of Harry Reilly. Finally, restraint would greatly simplify the cashing out of Lino's partnership equity. So he settled for the mental image of Fletcher's tortoise shell frames splattered and dripping with Lino's thick and lumpy green mucus. He envisioned Fletcher's preppy smugness dissolving into the pitiful sniveling of his inner being.

"You're right. I have come a long way. I resign."

Lino put his New York apartment up for sale. Within a week, he had rented a 1,000-square-foot studio apartment on Calle Luna in Old San Juan and moved in with a suitcase and a laptop. Lino called contacts at investment banks that he had met during merger deals. Larkin Capital, Lowell Partners, Eliot Ventures, and others. He explained the concept. They politely told him that he was in over his head, that this idea was just too ambitious, that the island could never get its act together to make Puerto Rico City happen.

"And Lino, you quit Ashton & Cavendish?" almost all of them asked. Some followed with "Are you OK?" Further emails to Lino's investment contacts from his personal g-mail account went unanswered.

Meanwhile, the island's economic news confirmed its relentless descent. Puerto Rico appeared in *The Economist* magazine behind Greece as the economy with the fastest shrinking GDP. Unemployment spiked. Drug trafficking crimes blackened the front covers of the island dailies. Plant closings followed their merciless trend. Local politicians continued their apoplectic tirades on Puerto Rico's ambiguous political relationship with the U.S. The Popular Democratic Party leaders, in favor of retaining Puerto Rico's unintelligible "commonwealth" territorial status, advocated for the resumption of unsustainable U.S. government tax breaks. Meanwhile, New Progressive Party leaders, seeking the wholly impossible grail of statehood, believed that full federal benefits, mostly food stamps and other welfare programs were the solution. No one offered a ballsy, self-reliant, transformational plan to lift the island from its dependence, inertia and descent.

During the 1950s and 1960s, Governor Luis Muñoz Marín had used federal tax incentives to lure manufacturers to the island. Without question, Puerto Rico experienced spectacular growth. However, in the 1970s, the first claws of globalization flared with the Middle East oil embargo. Then, as the fangs of foreign competition started biting into the necks of industrialized countries, Puerto Rico's population become complacent. Labor laws coddled workers and held employers hostage. Lawsuits for "political discrimination" found legal ground, when everyone had a political opinion. Official government idealism, built on tangible gains of the Muñoz Marín years, was also to blame. At first, Muñoz Marín argued that Puerto Rico and the U.S. had entered into a special "compact" that distinguished Puerto Rico from other U.S. territories. Then, in 1952, he orchestrated a constitutional convention, further seeking to clarify Puerto Rico's ambiguous political relationship with the U.S. Muñoz Marín needed a local popular vote before submitting the Puerto Rico constitution to the U.S. Congress for approval. In a pitch for votes, the Spanish version of the constitution described Puerto Rico as "Estado Libre Asociado," which in English literally means "Free Associated State." The added autonomy that this term implied helped garner a healthy majority of the local vote. However, the official English translation submitted to Congress used the term "Commonwealth of Puerto Rico."

In stark legal contrast to the "commonwealths" of Kentucky, Massachusetts, Pennsylvania, and Virginia, Puerto Rico remained a U.S. territory with millions of American citizens with no U.S. voting representation.

The U.S. Congress expressed no qualms about the "Commonwealth" term and its misleading translation of "Estado Libre Asociado," but it expressly rejected another vote-seeking clause that had been eagerly approved by the local populace. The rejected clause stated that basic human rights of Puerto Ricans include "The right of every person to obtain work." *If having a job were a basic right, who would put any effort into getting one?* — Lino thought.

On the other extreme, many statehood supporters proclaimed incessantly: "There is no one who can fix this," echoing the reputed dying words of Simón Bolívar, Spanish America's legendary freedom fighter, that "Latin America is ungovernable." The political confusion and psychic strain caused by years of conditioning and propaganda induced an island-centric perspective, the belief that the U.S. was watching, always there as a backup to bail Puerto Rico out of any mess it encountered. The truth was that few stateside Americans gave Puerto Rico any thought, and many would have trouble locating it on a map. For reasons that Lino still had not articulated, this national neglect fed on Lino's innards like ravenous maggots. *Other countries and races are surging ahead, while we are in decline.*

16 GETZING MONEY

For Lino, it was highly likely that at least one of the bidders for Roosevelt Roads would prevail, and the key portions of the property would be monopolized. Another exclusive enclave resort with security guards would emerge, or the mechanical pollution and blight of a port zone would scar the coast. Equally worse, several buyers might split it up for disparate uses, just as the local government proposed and had happened decades ago to the former Ramey Air Force base in Aguadilla on the northwest corner of Puerto Rico. Ramey was now carved up and fenced off into disjointed parts. The military housing was virtually gifted to local residents.

A few weeks remained until the deadline to qualify as a bidder, and Lino thought he had exhausted all funding sources. *"You quit Ashton & Cavendish?"* Lino kept hearing as he worked from the second-floor of 300-year-old cement apartment.

Lino was careful when he went outside. He had not called his mother Nereida to tell her he was on the island. He wore an assortment of hats and fake prescription glasses. Without this cover, he risked that romantic idealists of his past would recognize him and eat away at his valuable time. He affected an American accent when forced to speak Spanish in grocery stores, gas stations and restaurants. To mitigate total isolation, Lino chatted with tourists at the Caribe Hilton, the Conrad Vanderbilt and La Concha hotels.

Would I ever be able to go back to New York? Was I now damaged goods? – he thought to himself. Furthermore, what was in this for him? He had still not answered a basic question about the idea that drove him. How could he "monetize" Puerto Rico City for himself? An investment banker had once asked him this question straightaway, and Lino was stumped. He had not answered the question, because the question was fatal to the idea. At this early stage, narrow private gain and Puerto Rico City seemed mutually exclusive. The whole point was to create a diversified city where open competition spurred one-upmanship, innovation and even the greatness of his people. Why did he care about "his people?" There was a huge world out there for the taking. Why obsess over this tiny island? Was this an irrepressible genetic instruction to propagate his race? It was unlikely that he would get married and have children. He was too much of a player. Was this natural selection's way of helping his fellow Puerto Ricans prosper and multiply? The unexamined life might be worth living.

One evening after sending ten meticulously written emails bound for deletion by their recipients, Lino went to La Concha for a Don Q on the rocks. Arriving by taxi, he wore a pair of tinted gold-rimmed glasses and a black Chicago White Sox cap. He sat down at the bar. The bartender addressed him in English and took his order. As he reached for plantain chips in a bowl on the counter, Lino looked to his left. There next to him, stooped over his iPhone was Aaron Getz. As Getz yapped, saliva stretched and contracted furiously like rubber bands in the corners of his mouth. Lino felt the compulsion to hand him a napkin, less to protect Getz from electrocution than to subdue Lino's nausea.

Lino just listened as Getz yammered:

"I got back to the room and she was gone," Getz said with a Brooklyn accent. "No ... no ... for Christ's sake, she was with me for only an hour after landing! Can you believe it?... Don't answer that." Getz actually cracked a saliva-tangled smile. "Anyway, easy come, easy come. So, what's the word on the Atlas deal?"

After asking, Getz looked left then right. To Lino's relief, Getz grabbed a napkin and wiped his mouth. Getz then began to stare at Lino. Getz pulled the cell phone slightly away from his ear. He started squinting at Lino and then said into the phone. "Talk to you later."

Getz put down his iPhone, looked at Lino, and said: "Mendoza, you spic, I heard that they booted you out of Ashton & Cavendish."

"Booted is not accurate." Lino looked around to see who else had heard Getz.

"Well, you're not there anymore. Unless you're on to bigger and better things, why else does a lawyer leave Ashton & Cavendish?"

"Still pissed about the World Package deal?"

"You cost me a lot of money, spic." Getz bared the green patina on his two front teeth. Then, he ate the olive on a toothpick in his drink, Palo Viejo rum with soda.

Twenty years ago, the olive and the toothpick would have been up Getz's nose. Right there and then. Forget about a snot shot. Lino looked around again. Everybody in the bar seemed oblivious. Lino thought of his old Camaro, in mint condition, sheltered in the garage of his mother's home. The Glock 17 should still be safe and dry in a carrying case under the seat. In truth, the gun was going to be a family heirloom, but Lino could always buy a new equivalent. Lino looked at Getz in the face and, recalling a line by Norman Mailer, saw the word "spic" still smoking on Getz's lips.

"Tell you what." Lino consciously omitted his own epithet. "How about if I make it up to you?" Lino knew that Getz could easily find $65 million right in his shirt pocket. "But I don't want to discuss it in here. Let's take a walk outside."

"Go to hell." Getz said.

"No really, come on. I don't want to talk in here."

"Are you serious?" Getz asked.

"Yes. I'll take care of the drinks too." Lino threw two $20s on the counter. Getz did not thank him.

They walked out the glass doors, past the valet and bellhops dressed in white uniforms. They turned right, down the ramp in front of La Concha and towards La Ventana Al Mar, the beachside park on Ashford Avenue. The sun had just set. Lino tugged on his White Sox cap to stop it from flying off into the evening wind. They continued past the brown granite water sculpture and toward the ocean.

"Mendoza, this is very romantic, but what the hell are you going to talk to me about?"

Lino gave him the synopsis.

"Mendoza, I look for deals with immediate cash flow, but keep talking."

After Lino finished, Getz turned to Lino and said, "Okay, so now that you've told me all this, why would I need you?"

"Have you ever done a deal in Puerto Rico?"

Getz stared at Lino then nodded. "You'll hear from me if I'm interested. Give me your email and cell." Getz's pointy fingers worked quickly on his iPhone. Lino watched the stooped form turn and waddle back into La Concha.

17 LA CONQUISTA

♦

After Getz was gone, Lino headed toward the ocean walkway at the end of the park. He knew Getz was a long shot and potentially a huge burning bridge. By doing business with Getz, Lino could probably never go back to Ashton & Cavendish, even as a receptionist. But what were his options?   Ashton & Cavendish probably wouldn't take him back anyway.

Waves crashed up against the seawall and wet Lino's blue long-sleeve shirt. He got to the end of the walkway and looked out at the pale orange lights winking along the shoreline to the east. After a few minutes, he turned around, westward, and saw across the night water the festive glow of a cruise ship entering San Juan harbor. He got off the walkway, stepped onto the grass, passed the coconut trees, headed toward the beach behind La Concha, then cut a diagonal towards Sol y Luna, the open-air restaurant at the edge of the park. He sat down at a table for two, put the White Sox cap on the chair next to him, and checked his email on a Blackberry. Nothing. He ordered a Don Q on the rocks.

As Lino took a sip of his rum, a man and a woman holding hands approached the open table in front of him. The woman was a heart-stopper, even by the lofty aesthetic standards of Puerto Rico – a superpower of feminine beauty responsible for five Miss Universes.

Daisy Youngluck wore a gauze-thin lavender dress, cut just above the knee. The skirt was slit on the left side almost to her hip. Rob Swisher, her personal assistant, pulled out a chair with an NFL tackling arm. Daisy sat down, crossed her left leg over her right, revealing one of her gleaming racehorse thighs. Her toes, painted Bordeaux red, bounced gently in a white, four-inch heel sandal with a strap around her bronzed ankle. A diamond crucifix, glittering between magnificent upturned breasts, exalted the glory of the present above the naked promise of an afterlife. She put her right hand behind her delicate neck, gathered the middle of her long, glistening, brown hair and pulled it over her right shoulder. She turned slightly in Lino's direction.

"You're wet," she said.

"You should try it," Lino responded.

"Try eet?" Daisy asked.

Lino pointed toward the ocean walkway with the waves splashing over the top of the seawall.

Tipped off by her Spanish accent, he asked, "¿Y el grandote?" (And the big guy?).

"No as nadie" (He's nobody), she said.

Lino had already sensed that the man with an abnormally thick neck was only cover, and her signal was the universal one that so many men never understand: *"Move on me right now, or never."*

Daisy pushed a small glittering handbag across the table to Rob. Knowing that his duties had concluded for the night, Rob tucked the flashing pouch under his arm, failing miserably to make it look like a football. He got up without looking at Lino and walked away.

Lino knew that she had done this before. He guessed that she lived somewhere nearby, that she had spent several weeks admiring and lavishing her fabulous body in self-sufficient female solitude until the pangs of ovulation were too strong to resist. He could tell that she was accustomed to limited, compartmentalized encounters and nothing more. She had nullified one term of the popular but false male-female equation. She did not need a man for money, and she could afford protection on her own. Now, for Daisy, a man's sole purpose was to provide pleasure. When he wasn't fun anymore, she cast him off. Just like that.

Lino asked for two flutes of Korbel. Not Dom Perignon, not Veuve Clicquot, not Cristal, which were all available. It had been at least a month since Lino had enjoyed a woman's company, and she was gorgeous. He refrained from splurging because Lino's mother had taught him that oversolicitous male behavior was the pinnacle of weakness and stupidity.

Lino took the two flutes in one hand, walked up to her and said "Then let's go."

Daisy looked at Lino, who stood over her with a smile. Slowly, she got up from her chair. "By the way, my name is Daisy."

"Nice to meet you." Lino said.

"Yours?" Daisy asked.

He told her.

"Do I get one of those?"

"Do you want one?"

"Please."

Lino handed her a flute. They clinked glasses and walked on the grass toward the ocean walkway.

18 THE GIRASOL

"No, not from Chicago," Lino said to her in Spanish. "Just the hat." Lino was first impressed that Daisy noticed the White Sox cap, which he had left at the restaurant, a symbolic assurance that he would be back. "East Coast," he said.

Then she disclosed having once lived in New York City as well. Lino had an inkling who she was, but now it was confirmed. So he kept the exchanges primal and skin deep. The only other truly personal information that they shared was that Lino liked playing blackjack while she dabbled in baccarat. He kissed her and then licked off the ocean water that had splashed over the seawall onto her light chocolate shoulders.

"I bet you live close by," Lino said.

"I'm right over there," Daisy motioned with one of her delicious arms to The Girasol.

Lino put his hand around the other side of Daisy's narrow waist as they walked out of the park and directly across Ashford. The security guard at the Girasol remotely buzzed open the door and said, *"Buenas noches."* Daisy and Lino returned the greeting and entered an open elevator. Their bodies ascended 15 floors in a moist, hungry tangle. Before tumbling onto Daisy enormous bed, she pointed to a polished mahogany case on one side of the massive rattan headboard. Inside the case, organized like gourmet tea flavors, Lino found an assortment of condoms, oils, mints and chocolates. Lino sensed that on her side of the bed there was a means of contacting her thick-necked assistant if necessary. She probably had a weapon nearby as a final precaution. Lino couldn't blame her. She inspired multiple fertilizations, and some dolts simply can't take no for answer.

Just before sunrise, Lino put on his clothes and took a self-guided tour of the area outside Daisy's bedroom. As he passed a spacious, white-tiled open room next to the balcony, he saw four or five mocked-up, aerial photographs of Roosevelt Roads sitting on easels. Daisy had seized on this one too. She was planning one hotel and hundreds of upscale homes and villas – the smartest thing to do for a single owner.

The buyout of Daisy's cosmetics company, Diosa, had been a major transaction that, remarkably, Ashton & Cavendish had not worked on. While the business and legal press wrote about the deal, Daisy Youngluck's picture had stayed out of the news. That's why Lino had not immediately identified her. Once the deal closed, about two years ago, there was no further mention of her. The sales price of her privately owned company left little doubt that Daisy Youngluck had walked away with a couple billion dollars.

Lino realized that the only time he had ever come close to screwing a billionaire was when he "topped up" Aaron Getz in the World Package buyout. That near-hit earned him a partnership at Ashton & Cavendish. Now, this perfect strike earned him the knowledge that Getz would need to put up a lot more than $65 million to have a shot at the property.

Lino left before Daisy would have showed him out. Daisy had never served breakfast to an overnight visitor, but it crossed her mind this time. Also, she did not disturb the $500 in cash in Lino's pant pockets.

19 RECONQUISTA LTD.

_____

♦

As Lino left The Girasol, a different security guard smiled and then wrinkled his nose. "Lino? ... Is that you?" he asked.

"Sorry, sir. I don't speak Spanish." Lino had no idea who this man was, but he had obviously recognized him. This was getting difficult. Lino crossed Ashford and walked back to Sol y Luna. He found his White Sox cap still on the chair and ordered breakfast. A male waiter brought him a glass of tamarind juice, Yaucono Puerto Rican coffee and buttered *pan de agua*, the island's version of French baguette bread— but better.

"Next time, sir, please be so kind as to bring back the champagne glasses yourself," the waiter told him in English. Lino had left the two empty flutes on the dry side of the seawall.

"Certainly, my friend." Lino knew not to sass a Puerto Rican waiter. Lino included a $20 tip for his trouble. He still had a couple of years before this pace of spending would run him dry.

In the early morning sun, Lino rode a taxi back to Old San Juan. He napped until noon in his studio apartment on Calle Luna. His arms, back and legs were unusually fatigued. His left knee was slightly swollen. Last night's action had not been confined only to Daisy's bed. They had roamed freely through much of the 1,000 square feet of her bedroom. Tufiño, Botello, and Hernández-Cruz paintings on the walls needed to be straightened. He and Daisy had passionately rearranged expensive rattan chairs, a table and a sofa. They had even pushed a sturdy Luis Torruella sculpture out of its proper appointment.

Rolling out of his bed, Lino checked his Blackberry. A starred email in bold simply said, "Getz." He wanted to meet Lino at La Concha at 5 p.m. Lino showered and then read the local papers. There was nothing reported about the land auction. As five approached, he called a taxi and arrived at the hotel on time. He covered his head with a brown crushable fedora. He wore the tinted glasses, a blue blazer, dark khaki slacks, and Ferragamo loafers. Lino saw Getz's curly gray sides and bald spot in the upper seating area facing one of the two heated Jacuzzi pools. Getz's skinny fingers turned off his iPhone as Lino approached.

"Okay, Mendoza, as I said, it's not my usual thing." Getz was interested. "You put together the entity papers. You're getting ten percent of the stock and net after I flip it."

"Ten point one percent." Lino instinctively interjected, even though he knew that Getz's opening ten percent offer was extraordinarily generous for someone not putting in any money.

"Okay, ten-point-one percent," The "top up" card had already been played.

"And what do you mean by 'flip it.'" Lino said.

Getz scratched his nose. "Your basic idea is OK, but the payback period needs to be realistic. We're going to get the whole tortilla, the 2,900 acres and then the rest of the base when it's put up for sale. We'll lease out pieces to different resort operators. Then we'll sell our rights within three years."

Lino thought about it. The site needed infrastructure starting with the airport and the rail system, then central design and planning. These details could come later. Besides, Lino's options were shrinking.

"Sounds reasonable."

"My CFO at Haifa Partners is going to run the checkbook." Getz said. "Show me the corporate papers and start filling out the bid forms. I will kick in an extra $500 an hour for your legal work."

Lino's stomach turned. *Getz's ten percent initial offer and now legal fees? Way too generous* – Lino thought.

"I can't do that." Lino said. "I'm not going to be your lawyer on this. I'm an investor."

"Whatever," Getz said. "Just get the papers done. And, by the way, I already know that Daisy Youngluck is going to throw in some of her cosmetics deal money into this. There are some other players too. So I'm probably going to have to kick in more cabbage. I'm sure you already knew that. One other thing, so that there's no interference, you're going to have to cozy up to … umm … the locals." Uncharacteristically, Getz had edited his speech.

Getz was definitely interested.

The broad outline sounded good to Lino, too good, but this was going to be in writing, and Getz was going to sign in his personal capacity.

"What do you want to call the company?" Lino asked.

"That's up to you." Getz's skinny fingers started poking his iPhone.

The next day, Lino prepared articles of incorporation. Lino included an anti-dilution provision that would stop Getz from issuing more shares and reducing Lino's 10.1 percent. Lino was not going to get "topped up" on his own deal. He prepared a separate shareholders' agreement with a voting trust giving Lino an equal blocking right to prevent any amendment to the articles. Getz emailed the papers to his personal attorney, a typically anonymous corporate lawyer in Manhattan. Getz met Lino at the business conference center of the La Concha and signed. Lino rode a taxi to the Puerto Rico secretary of state's office on one end of Plaza de Armas in Old San Juan and filed the articles of incorporation for Reconquista Ltd.

20 THE AUCTION

Reed Savage had stopped going to the Bahamas because winter temperatures could be nearly freezing. As for the Dominican Republic, Savage had several reasons for no longer going there to escape the Connecticut winters. Once, he had won about $70,000 from a casino in Punta Cana on the east coast. He had driven 130 miles from the capital, Santo Domingo, in a rental car. When the $100 black chips had mushroomed in front of him, the blackjack dealers and the pit bosses began glaring at Savage and whispering to each other. He cashed in his chips and started the three-hour drive back that night to Santo Domingo. Every headlight behind him threatened a major inconvenience. Then his car broke down. Savage had to walk in the dark along

Puerto Rico City

the side of the road to wake up a local mechanic at his home gas station. He sweated off a meaningful portion of his body fluids while the mechanic replaced the battery. The cost: $500. Then, after arriving in the capital, Savage had to shell out another $1,000 to two armed men in military uniforms who started interrogating him about his perfectly valid U.S. passport just before his departure from the Santo Domingo airport.

By comparison, Puerto Rico was an easy domestic trip. No U.S. passport required. No customs inspection. Whenever he visited, Savage stood a little taller. Besides his being six-four and taller than most of its residents, Puerto Rico brought back youthful memories of an early, unblemished score. He liked to think that the Caribe Hilton had closed its historical casino in 1998 because of him. Savage had badly hemorrhaged the blackjack tables. Shortly thereafter, it seemed, the entire pit crew and all the dealers he recognized were gone. Unconfirmed rumors had it that the casino union and other troublemakers retaliated so severely that the management could never restaff it. The Caribe Hilton & Casino became just the Caribe Hilton.

Even now, without a casino, Savage still enjoyed the open tropical garden ambiance, the semi-private calm-water beach, the old Spanish fort – San Jerónimo – connected to the east side of the property. Before opening in 1949, the hotel, built on a long-term ground lease from the Puerto Rico government, had been blasted as fantasy. Almost sixty years later, truth be told, the chic and historic lodging on the wind-swept promontory was still fabulous.

Savage sat splay-legged on a lounge chair on the beach facing a protected inlet. A swim-up raft floated a hundred yards away in front of him. He wore black Hugo Boss swim trunks. Large brown-tinted Dolce & Gabbana sunglasses hung on his nose that was smeared with white sunscreen. He held a glass of Palo Viejo rum with soda.

"You want one?"

"I want an olive in mine," Getz said, as he waddled over in red swim trunks. His matching button-down short-sleeve shirt, open at his white belly, looked like part of a bowling team uniform. Getz plopped down on a lounge chair next to Savage. Savage flagged over a waiter from the cabañas behind them. The waiter brought Getz his drink.

"Just think," Savage said, "Hawaii scooped up $12 billion from visitors last year – even without any gaming. Puerto Rico has only done a quarter of that. And the flight here is a cinch compared to the haul and time-zone changes cross country and over the Pacific. Sooner or later, the locals are going to figure this out."

"Nervous?" Getz asked.

"Are you kidding?"

"So you talked to her."

"Yeah, yeah, we talked and a little more than that." Savage said. "She's got a hell of a place, too, overlooking the park and the ocean. Funny thing happened. When I got back here, about a thousand dollars were missing from my pants. It was worth it though," Savage lifted up his sunglasses and winked at Getz. "And, best of all, she's in."

Getz had helped Savage in the "mezzanine" days of The Deer Hunter Hotel & Casino. Making the jump from 1,000 to 3,000 hotel rooms required a good chunk of cash, and Getz made it possible, albeit at a ridiculous premium. Getz was also instrumental in Savage's baffling, yet certified genealogical proof of his pure Apache bloodline. Through its Oakland office, Haifa Partners had helpful self-directed contacts within the California Demographic Registry who could print highly convincing counterfeit birth certificates. Savage still felt the rub from the cost of it all and didn't particularly like Getz, but practical circumstances overrode emotion.

"What about the Russian kid?" Getz asked.

"You mean Estonian. He lived in Russia for a while and speaks Russian, but he's Estonian."

"Thanks for the history lesson. What about him?"

"I'm sure he's listening. I see him in the restaurant," Savage said as he looked almost straight ahead at the calm water. "Rubelkov, why don't you just come over? Bring a hat too. The sun is blazing." Savage waived his right arm sideways over his head as though Rubelkov were only a few yards away from his side.

Puerto Rico City

21 A MARTÍNEZ

♦

Rubelkov sat behind the tall windows in the Caribe Hilton restaurant overlooking the beach where Getz and Savage sat in the distance. A pen-shaped object rested on his right ear, mostly hidden by his black curly hair. With a napkin in his lap, Rubelkov used a knife and fork to eat a *medianoche* sandwich – pork, pickles, cheese and mayonnaise on a sweet yellow bun. He drank a *martínez* – white grapefruit juice, dark rum and ice. The exquisitely fermented caramel taste of Ron del Barrilito hovered finely in his mouth after each sip. He had run into Savage and Getz during a tour of Roosevelt Roads a few weeks before. Getz had entered Roosevelt Roads for an inspection tour with Savage.

Savage had obtained a special pass by submitting his bid papers and $3 million earnest deposit. Getz had wasted no time.

A bidding war was moronic, and Rubelkov's transshipment depot made a lot more sense if it could be located, not on Roosevelt Roads on the east coast, but toward west side of the island. Routes would be at least two hundred miles shorter for cargo vessels coming to and from the U.S. that used the Panama Canal. The abandoned oil refining site at Peñuelas toward the southwest coast was a perfect substitute. That eyesore of rusted machinery, petroleum tanks, and pipes had sat nearly idle for years. The Puerto Rico government would shower Rubelkov with tax breaks, giving no thought to the deepening fiscal hole it had dug for the island's inhabitants by doing this over the years. The wonderful myth diagrammed by the Laffer curve and made famous and plausible by Ronald Reagan – that lower taxes paid for themselves – did just as much damage in Puerto Rico. The island's debt burden was well over 100 percent of its GDP.

But, as Getz and Savage suggested, Peñuelas would work fine for Rubelkov. Plus, the anonymity of a secure Puerto Rican-style Russian dacha in the mountains just inland from Peñuelas was equally attractive to him.

Rubelkov had enough money to run up the bidding for Roosevelt Roads. This had a value all to its own. With one look at Rubelkov, Getz and Savage knew this. Yet it was Savage who was keen to state-of-the-art surveillance and hacking. Savage knew not to let Rubelkov touch him, and he assumed that Rubelkov could catch every word somehow. On the way out of Roosevelt Roads, Getz and Savage approached Rubelkov. They took him out to dinner at Augusto's in Miramar. They talked.

After receiving Savage's wireless invitation from the beach, Rubelkov paid cash for his *medianoche* breakfast, refreshed his *martínez*, and walked outside toward Getz and Savage. Rubelkov arrived hatless but fully clothed in jeans, a light green Fernando Pena short-sleeve shirt, and Playero sandals. His skin was pasty white.

"Take some sunscreen." Savage motioned with his head to the table next to him.

"Thanks." Rubelkov took the bottle and smudged the white lotion on his nose and forehead.

"I did not see Wen Kashing this morning." Getz said.

"He's going to work it out on his own with her." Rubelkov said. "As long as we get our end, we don't really care, do we?"

"Still, I want to know. I'm putting up some real money, even it's much less than the land is worth," said Getz.

22 DUOPOLY

♦

Wen had tried walking into the casino at La Concha while smoking a Boriqua Puro. The security guard stopped him and pointed at the cigar. Wen leaned back with his relaxed shoulders.

"Next time I'll consider Las Vegas," Wen said.

"Sorry, sir."

"It's quite all right my friend. You do not make the rules."

He smiled condescendingly at the security guard, dropped the lit cigar in an ashtray and left it smoking by the door. He continued into the casino. Wen wondered if there was an equivalent of Macau's garment district in Puerto Rico where he might hire some help, not for this security-guard fellow, who was harmless and just doing his job, but maybe for someone else. He sat down at the $100 minimum bet baccarat table and bought $5,000 in chips. He was the only player, just what he preferred.

After Wen lost and won a few hands, Daisy Youngluck walked in with Rob Swisher. Rob towered by her side as he pulled out a chair for her at the baccarat table next to Wen. Wen was about to stop and take his chips until he got the full view. Daisy crossed a tantalizing, smooth leg, and a spiked four-inch heel just grazed Wen's knee. The sparkling crucifix hanging from her delicate neck bounced between two mighty crests. She bought in for $10,000.

"I used to be a believer, too," Wen said.

"I don't believe in anything. I just like the way eet looks." Daisy pinched the crucifix, then twirled it as she watched Wen's eyes. He kept his eyes fixed on hers. He passed the test.

"You must make a living at this game." Daisy said. She noticed the Patek Philippe watch, the durable stitching of his black Testoni shoes.

"That's a good guess, but not exactly like this," Wen said.

She knew who he was.

Daisy handed Rob her black velvet Hermès pouch, and the former football player headed off to his locker room. *He's overpaid* – Daisy thought to herself.

Wen bought $5,000 more in chips and the game stopped being one against the dealer and really just a game against her. Daisy, however, lost her chips in a hurry, and then feigned a sad face.

"I'll tell you what to do differently. Join me out on the patio."

Wen cashed in his chips, $12,000, and spent several minutes completing a currency transaction report. He folded the $100 bills evenly in the front pockets of his pleated pants. She pretended not to notice. They walked out of the casino, into the glass and marble lobby of the hotel and past the bar. They continued beyond the first pool and down the stairs, to the right, toward a second infinite horizon pool facing the beach. Wen was relaxed and confident. She liked him too. They ended up on the fifteenth floor of The Girasol.

After healthy cardiovascular conversation, Wen and Daisy discussed the aerial photographs of Roosevelt Roads in the room just next to her balcony. Before this discussion, imaginary tender remembrances of her father Stanley did not prevent Daisy from sneaking a few grand out of Wen's pockets. After Wen returned to his room at the Conrad Vanderbilt that night, he noticed the missing money but shrugged it off. Daisy would get most of the hotel and all the land to sell for the private homes and villas. Wen would get the premium upscale hotel suites on the top floors, a penthouse, and the entire casino.

23 THE AWARD

The deadline for the bids arrived.

"Mendoza, this deal is a lot dicier than I thought," said Getz on the phone. "The goddamn Puerto Rico government won't back off from the reuse plan. It could take ten years before they drop the crap about schools, science parks, and low-income housing. I'm not risking more than $66 million, and that's it."

From his Calle Luna studio apartment, Lino checked the account using his laptop. The wire transfer for the certified funds was real. Reconquista Ltd. was good for $66 million, just one million more than the $65 million minimum. Getz was at least following through with more than the minimum. Getz could have refused to fund the company altogether. Thus, accusations of bad faith against Getz would look legally implausible. Plus, Lino had put up no money of his own. His contribution was the idea for Puerto Rico City. Yet, how much was his idea worth? Without the land and strategic implementation, Puerto Rico City was probably worth nothing. For Puerto Rico City to work it needed comprehensive planning to ensure that the precious land did not end up as an incoherent hodgepodge or a short-sighted tool for monopoly interests. A lawsuit against Getz would probably get Lino just the value of his time for due diligence and for preparing the front-end paperwork required to submit the bid.

Yet something larger did not square. The $66 million was a drop in the hat for Getz. On the scale of his normal investment plays, $66 million was next to nothing. Also, Getz was giving up too soon, and Getz was anything but a quitter. He was used to getting kicked around, knocked down, and rejected, and then getting right back up.

Lino pessimistically submitted Reconquista's bid, while fully expecting that the 2,900 acres would receive a bid of a billion dollars or more. However, Daisy Youngluck's company, Makeover Enterprises, got all 2,900 acres for only $66.5 million. Dozens of other firms had submitted bids.

There was little doubt now. The 10.1 per cent stake that Getz had given to Lino had not been too rich, because it was never going to payoff. Lino knew that it would take a federal antitrust lawsuit for bid rigging naming Getz, Daisy and several John Does to find out exactly what had happened. The cost and the time would be prohibitive. Lino could never carry that load on his own. He ruminated for days in his apartment on Calle Luna. Getz emailed a copy of a filing with the Puerto Rico secretary of state dissolving Reconquista Ltd. since its corporate purpose had expired.

The details of what Lino suspected resided in several hidden events. Days before the bid deadline, Wen and Daisy had privately spoken with Getz and Savage. Getz and Savage then spoke with Rubelkov. Rubelkov hacked into the bidder registry and helped Getz and Savage to arrange more meetings with other bidders. The land would go to Wen and Daisy, but in the name of Daisy's company, Makeover Enterprises. More direct involvement by Wen, with his Chinese connections, risked delay and review by the U.S. Foreign Investment Committee. Yet, for practical purposes, the entire property would be Wen's and Daisy's – a one-hotel and casino town with private mansions and expensive villas to be sold off in stages: The same tired and disastrous development model that stunted Puerto Rico's potential. Wen and Daisy could make their money with limited competition. Getz, Savage, Rubelkov and others would also get what they wanted. These three would also each receive "cooperation fees" of $500 million from Wen and Daisy for keeping the bids close to the $65 million minimum. Finally, Savage and several operators from Las Vegas and Atlantic City, who had submitted bids, would kill the idea of a mega-entertainment city in Puerto Rico. The strictly upscale and exclusive resort, planned by Wen and Daisy, would have a narrow appeal and would not threaten margins in Las Vegas, Atlantic City or southwestern Connecticut, where Savage had his business.

24 THE TEAM

The greatest achievement that Lino could claim from his quixotic venture was a night at The Girasol, where he thought that he had tilted a billionaire when the reverse was true. Lino envisioned his future, back in New York City, as a storefront sole practitioner handling child support cases in Spanish Harlem. He imagined Burton Fletcher at Ashton & Cavendish gloating behind his tortoise shell glass frames.

Lino left his studio apartment on Calle Luna without the hat and glasses. He walked the narrow sidewalks of Old San Juan. He rode a public bus to the campus of the University of Puerto Rico in Río Piedras. He began reconnecting with his past. He called his mother Nereida and told her he was back, but that it could be several months before he visited. It seemed that at every street corner, someone stopped Lino to catch up on where he had been and what he had done. At first, it was tedious and draining. Then he started to control the subject and hone his message, the English translation of which went something like this:

"They're stealing the land on Roosevelt Roads."

"Where?"

"Ceiba, the old naval base. It's our last chance. Let's build a new city there....

"No, no, – the empty military houses should not be given away to local residents. We need to tear them down and build a new city, starting with a clean slate."

At night in his bed, Lino's anger permutated and hardened. He woke up one morning and wrote a detailed account in English about the bidding process. He signed and dated it under penalty of perjury. He sent counterpart originals to the U.S. Department of Justice, the Federal Trade Commission, and the FBI. Solomón Ortega, the U.S. Attorney for the federal district of Puerto Rico, began an investigation. Within weeks, the U.S. Navy halted the transfer process of the 2,900 acres to Makeover Enterprises, then entirely annulled the auction.

Lino began receiving a barrage of emails and phone messages from Getz, asking Lino to return his call. Proof of the calls clinched Getz's status as an unindicted co-conspirator in the case against Daisy Youngluck and Wen Kashing. Through his Brooklyn attorney, Getz "vehemently denied the allegations," but business for his company, Haifa Partners, began to suffer. The bad press about the bid-rigging case hurt Getz's credibility in proxy contests for public companies and even in private deals.

Puerto Rico federal authorities could not find Daisy until a female owner of a jewelry boutique in Condado made a citizen's arrest of Daisy for shoplifting. Daisy had tried to steal a new chain for her diamond crucifix. It takes a woman to catch a woman. After a top New York criminal defense lawyer flew in to the rescue, Daisy was let out on a $1-million bond, which she wrote from her personal checkbook in one of her many designer purses. Then she disappeared. Rob Swisher, her personal assistant, moved to Las Vegas and got a gig as a male dancer while looking for something more substantial.

Wen Kashing slipped out of the island on a private jet from Isla Grande airport in Miramar. He returned to Macau and paid the $250 million subconcession fee to operate the gaming tables at the Emperor King. He had employees maintain his stock of Boriqua Puro cigars. Wen made sure that the appropriate authorities in Macau ignored U.S. extradition requests. After all, bid rigging in Macau was far less than even a petty offense; it was the lauded sport of savvy businessmen.

Not mentioned by name in the indictment, Reed Savage made his way back to Connecticut and lay low. Billy Wildfoot and Chet Lighthouse, his Native American "consultants" became the faces of The Deer Hunter Hotel & Casino while Savage studied spreadsheets in the back offices. Charging another ridiculous premium for his proprietary connections at the California Demographic Registry, Getz helped Savage's Native American blood drop back to 20 percent in case anyone started digging.

Rubelkov returned to Estonia after receiving the first $100 million of the $500 million "cooperation fee" from Wen and Daisy. Daisy and Wen were able to stop the other payments to Savage and Getz, but once Rubelkov obtained the originating bank account information, a few computer strokes by Rubelkov made the transaction for his portion irreversible. In any event, Rubelkov was concerned less with federal authorities and Interpol than with Russian oligarch Mikhail Petrovich, who laid claim to at least half of Rubelkov's lifetime earnings, whatever the source. The tracking chip on Petrovich's signet ring helped Rubelkov evade sniper fire on two occasions. Special imports of Puerto Rican rum kept Rubelkov warm and preserved his inherited composure.

There was no indication that any of them knew that Lino had triggered the investigation and indictments. Yet U.S. Attorney Ortega arranged for Lino to have plain clothes bodyguards at the expense of the federal government. Lino kept them busy.

Lino went back to visit the political science classes at the University of Puerto Rico. Many of his former professors, now grayer and heavier, still taught in the same classrooms. Proud of his Ivy League credentials and New York law firm experience, they gave Lino floor time. Instead of the abstract speeches on the dialectical forces that would erode capitalism, Lino's marching plans were different:

"Let's build Puerto Rico City."

He actually used the term "Ciudad Borinquen," which played better with his audience. "Ciudad" was the Spanish word for city. "Borinquen" was the indigenous Taíno name for Puerto Rico. Puerto Ricans often referred to themselves as *boricuas*. "Ciudad Borinquen" would be the name in Spanish, but for the business world, it would have to be "Puerto Rico City," Lino explained. He also foresaw variations of the name, PR City, Party City, evolving over time. Thus, Lino revised a page from the playbook of former governor Luis Muñoz Marín in his campaign to approve the 1952 constitution of the "Estado Libre Asociado," which was officially and deceptively translated into English as the "Commonwealth of Puerto Rico."

Lino's speeches went more or less like this:

"Globalization is here. It's not going away. The days of subsidies are over. If we want jobs, we will have to invent our own. If we're are going to build anything, let's build a dozen fifty-story hotels that are hurricane-proof, sports arenas, theaters, monorail systems, and tropical parks.

"Let's have our own airline.

"If we're going to make anything, let's make good memories for all of our guests and visitors. That means we smile and say thank you. That means we pick up trash, even if it's not our own.

"Puerto Rico City will compete with Las Vegas, Atlantic City, and Orlando. We have been sitting on gold and diamonds all this time and did not know it. Let other countries pollute themselves to death with toxic industries. We will be clean, fun and exciting. And, most of all, cool. Supremely cool. A tropical island like ours is the most precious and valuable resource that the Earth has to offer." Lino had exaggerated. One of the keys was that Puerto Rico was just three to four hours from the U.S. mainland.

"But we have to make Puerto Rico City our own. New cities are being built every day, new cities with renewable energy, ultra-safe construction, and clean transportation without cars.

"No cars. I repeat. No cars.

"Former President Clinton ... yes ladies, I know ... I know ... proposed that Puerto Rico become a model for complete energy independence. Forget about a gas pipeline that's going to cut a scar through the middle of the mountains. This island of flat roofs will be the land of solar panels and smart wind farms.

"Not only will Puerto Rico City be energy independent, it will be fiscally independent and environmentally friendly. You watch, instead of us asking the United States for help, the United States will ask us for help.

"We must act now because the window is about to close. Say yes to Puerto Rico City! Say yes to Puerto Rico City! Say yes!"

25 THE GOVERNMENT

♦

Lino wrote a ten-page manifesto on Puerto Rico City. Students, especially young attractive women, helped circulate thousands of copies. Lino organized outdoor meetings in the University of Puerto Rico amphitheater and sports stadium. Students began arriving by the hundreds and then the thousands. Lino led marches at the University's main campus in Río Piedras, then the regional campuses in Mayagüez, on the west coast, and Humacao on the southeast coast. Puerto Rico City started appearing on websites and social media. The island newspapers and television stations began to interview Lino again.

Despite the popular demonstrations, Puerto Rico governor Manuel Casado responded half-heartedly. Casado knew about Lino's past as a nationalist agitator. So Casado only modified the reuse plan and kept the scale limited and subdued. Tourism was now the emphasis. But the proposal reverted to the same failed development model: A single-owner, upscale casino and hotel with only 2,500 rooms surrounded by private homes – essentially what Daisy Youngluck and Wen Kashing had been planning.

To Lino, the timing could be spun to suggest that government may have received inducements from Wen and Daisy, that this change of the reuse plan had been a *fait accompli* that was only disclosed after the criminal investigation was announced and the indictments filed.

Moreover, Casado had won the last gubernatorial election by only a few hundred votes, so he was vulnerable. Wall Street was in flames. Bear Sterns and Lehman Brothers had collapsed. The financial crisis went pandemic. Puerto Rico unemployment ramped even higher.

Separately, the legally fixed $70,000 annual salary for the governor of Puerto Rico helped spur rumors about Casado's uncanny ability to maintain his impeccable appearance, corporate haircuts and designer suits. On several occasions, press photographs caught an open suit jacket. Armani, Versace and Valentino labels started showing up on local Puerto Rican web blogs. One blogger posted a cartoon spoof of Casado with a boardroom haircut, sporting an Armani tuxedo and walking out of a limousine into the Kodak Theatre in Hollywood. The spoof had him nominated as director of "Best Documentary" on the layoffs of thousands of Puerto Rican government workers. Lino thought that Casado's reputation as a callous "pretty boy" would start to crest at just the right time.

A hundred thousand signatures to place Lino on the ballot for the next gubernatorial elections were easy pickings. Even members of Casado's own party sought to recruit Lino for a position in the cabinet or as senator-at-large, just to remove any threat to Casado's reelection. Casado's main opposition party headed by Gil Pedraza made similar overtures. Lino also turned down what was left of the handful of nationalist parties, now reduced to fringe groups. The same ground forces of young, beautiful female students fanned out to cities, towns, and neighborhoods to elect Lino as governor of Puerto Rico for his new Borinquen Party.

Casado, Pedraza and the other party candidates tried to ridicule Lino for having no position on the island's political relationship with the United States. Lino welcomed the attacks and responded:

"Look at where the status debate has gotten us: Nowhere.

"We've been arguing about the status for more than a 100 years, and nothing has happened. It is not the local government's job to decide this issue. Only the U.S. Congress can decide. You can look it up in the U.S. Constitution, Article 4, Section 3.

"So it is pointless for Puerto Rico's parties and the local government to spend so much time, money and effort on the status question. If you want to change the status, send your requests to the U.S. Congress.

"I will set up an independent status commission. And each year, everyone can file their status requests with the commission. The commission will then send your requests, tabulated and organized, to the U.S. Congress, which is the only body that can decide the status issue.

"It makes no sense to vote for a local party based on the status question. Again, only the U.S. Congress can help you.

Puerto Rico City

"And you statehooders, especially, don't be surprised if the U.S. denies Puerto Rico statehood, even if an overwhelming majority of us wants it.

"So I say to you: Vote for a party based on its specific plans to make your lives better now, regardless of what happens to Puerto Rico's status.

"And my plan to build Puerto Rico City has more potential and promise than anything else the other parties are offering.

"Do you really want more food stamps to solve your problems? Do you really want the government to give large corporations more tax breaks so that they pay less taxes than you do? Do you really want more polluting industries to buy up what's left of the open land and leave behind rusted heaps of waste once the tax breaks run out?

"Puerto Rico is being forgotten and ignored. Do you want attention from the U.S.? Do you want attention from the world? Then let's build Puerto Rico City.

"We need to act on a big scale. We need a project with global dimensions and transformational impact. Let's stop the focus on small and marginal improvements. Let's wake up to the world economy, admit our shortcomings and embrace our strengths. Poetry and literature are great things to know, but we need engineers and architects to build 30,000 new hotel rooms and performing arts and sports arenas that can take on hurricanes. We need management and financial experts. We need singers, dancers, and, yes, beauty queens to entertain and make people happy.

"Our main export will be good memories. And best of all, we're going to be paid well for this.

"We need to start from a clean slate. We need to start building a new economy with Puerto Rico City."

Lino waxed Lincolnesque: "Few will remember and many will forget the inauguration of a single exclusive hotel, the opening of a new surface road for more traffic, or the new extension of the cafeteria of a public elementary school. But how would the world fail to notice the creation of a new great city devoted to a single task, the first of its kind in the Western Hemisphere?

"Gleaming modern cities, Dubai and Doha, are rising in the Middle East. Songdo is pushing the edge of urban design and technology in South Korea. Macau is receiving tens of billions of dollars a year for new buildings and infrastructure to give people what they ultimately want: A good time. And a good time is what Puerto Rico and Puerto Ricans are best at – having and showing other people a good time.

"No, no … feel no shame in saying that. A good time is what we as a human race are all after.

"Vote for me, and I will lead us to a good time – a time that we will earn and a time that we deserve."

26 MADAME SECRETARY

♦

Casado and Pedraza dug into Lino's past. Ashton & Cavendish received inquiries, presumably sent by Puerto Rican newspapers. Amazingly but perhaps predictably, Burton Fletcher, on behalf of the firm, expressed "Ashton & Cavendish's strong support and best wishes for Lino Mendoza in his campaign for governor of Puerto Rico." Lino imagined Burton salivating behind his tortoise shell eyeglass frames in hopes of future Puerto Rico triple-tax-exempt bond deals and legal advisory contracts. It's the way the game is played. But Burton would get nothing profitable for the firm, if Lino had any say in the matter.

Casado and Pedraza unearthed pictures of Lino being arrested on the University campus during the tuition protest days. They also produced written statements, though marred by misspellings and grammatical errors, from several members of Lino's childhood burglary crew. A picture of Lino's stolen Camaro with an expired tag from 1985 appeared in one of the island dailies. An account that Lino had used a Glock 17 handgun found its way into a television interview of someone whose only identification was "Papo."

This political dirt only made Casado and Pedraza look desperate. The arrests were recast into abuses of police power to muzzle Lino's First Amendment right to free speech on matters of public interest. The burglaries were dismissed as overblown horseplay in private homes to which Lino had been duly invited. Lino effectively characterized the stolen Camaro as an extended teenage joyride. As for the Glock 17, who hadn't practiced shooting at natural targets in the Puerto Rican outdoors, given the paucity of regulation firing ranges?

Lino won by a landslide election victory and was inaugurated as governor of Puerto Rico on January 2, 2009.

As his first official act, Lino chose his mother, Nereida Mendoza as secretary of state, the second highest officer and successor to the governor. Lino anticipated the controversy, but there was similar precedent at a much higher level. In 1961, President John F. Kennedy had selected his younger brother Robert to be Attorney General of the United States. The Kennedys were huge in Puerto Rico. President Kennedy had been the last U.S. president to make an official visit to the island. Less than one year after taking office, President Kennedy and the First Lady arrived, rode in a motorcade through Old San Juan, and spent the night at the governor's mansion, La Fortaleza, as Muñoz Marín's guests. After his death, the president's youngest brother U.S. Senator Ted Kennedy regularly visited the island and enjoyed having cocktails in Old San Juan with another former governor. One of the bedrooms in La Fortaleza is named the Kennedy Bedroom.

In addition, Nereida had been an ace lawyer and judge who could make the legislative leaders look silly. Before the voting, Nereida worked the Puerto Rico Senate and House party elders who headed the confirmation hearings. She wore appropriate attire, snug to her still attractive figure: a red dress with a plunging neckline covered just-so-much by a matching neck scarf. And she insisted, playfully, even before her confirmation that she be addressed as "Madame Secretary." Several of the Senate and House members had hopelessly tried to keep up with Nereida in law school and grudgingly respected her unrewarded intellect. Lino's female supporters blanketed the steps of El Capitolio, the iconic legislative building overlooking the Atlantic. For days, they chanted "Nereida, Nereida." She was confirmed by a slim majority.

From La Fortaleza, Lino immediately went to work on the cornerstone of his administration: The redirection of the island's economy and the creation of Puerto Rico City.

He began by setting the tone in Old San Juan. At sunrise for an hour each day, he and every member of his cabinet, dressed in jeans and work boots, picked up trash on sidewalks, gutters and cobblestone streets. Then they started traveling in a caravan of vehicles to the beaches in Condado and Isla Verde. Newspaper and television cameras watched as they picked up every trace of litter in their path. Men, women and children from all walks started to join them. Soon, during the first hour of sunlight each day, every able-bodied person went out of their home and picked up. Television commercials, bumper stickers, Twitter messages started to appear, saying in Spanish: "Did you pick up today?"

Vendors of aluminum and glass containers collected an extra nickel upon each sale and paid back the nickel for each return. Prisoners incarcerated for simple drug possession were released on condition of providing two hours per day of community hygiene and beautification service for each day of their sentence. Abandoned building owners were given deadline notices to paint and clean. After the deadline, their buildings were demolished and replaced with fresh grass and ferns.

Lino's televised addresses called out to every one to "Smile and be friendly to our guests. They are family. We still don't have room for all them, but Puerto Rico City is coming."

27 OKINAWA

♦

On January 20, 2009, weeks after Lino became governor, Makoto ("Mack") Okinawa took office as the first Asian American President of the United States. The outgoing administration handed him the U.S. economy raging in a ball of flames as it rolled into an abyss. Resenting their loss of the White House, Unicrats in the U.S. Congress first attacked Okinawa as a puppet of rising Asian nations. Then they proclaimed an austerity crusade with no explanation as to how less government spending would mitigate the collapsing economy. Millions of unemployed consumers had stopped spending. Now, as if to stimulate the economy, government would stop spending.

The sale of Roosevelt Roads and the costs needed to maintain the former base by the federal government played into the austerity theme. The U.S. Navy announced another auction, this time of the entire thirteen square-mile site. For Lino, the opportunities and risks were present in equal measures. The shine and momentum of his speedy rise to the governor's office would eventually wear down. The statehood and commonwealth parties, who controlled the Puerto Rico legislature, would begin to obstruct him. Even if the Puerto Rico government could control the zoning and use of the land from Roosevelt Roads through local legislation after the sale, a change in Puerto Rico's government could simply reverse course. To build Puerto Rico City, stability and certainty were essential.

Meanwhile, the Unicratic wing of the U.S. Congress, led by Senator Rhett Neckles of Oklahoma and Representative Andy Spandeport of West Virginia, went line by line through the federal budget. Puerto Rico appeared as a perfect, juicy cost-cutting target. This was true, especially since Puerto Rico had no vote for President, no vote in the U.S. House or Senate. Moreover, Puerto Rico residents paid no federal income taxes on Puerto Rico-source income. The island territory could be treated almost with impunity.

While Lino had seen the federal cuts coming, he also contemplated a starker fate: Forced independence from the U.S. The rabid anti-immigrant sentiment wafting across the country was really a proxy against Hispanics. Unless Puerto Rico held some lasting value for the U.S., it would eventually be cut loose. For Lino, the closing of the Roosevelt Roads naval base swallowed the last morsel of Puerto Rico's military importance. Puerto Ricans had received their U.S. citizenship in the spring of 1917, when the U.S. needed thousands of fighting men to meet the call for World War I. But now, there were more Puerto Ricans living on the U.S. mainland than on the island. Also, with drones and long-range missiles, the utility of blue-water navies could be questioned. Thus, the island may have dwindled to nothing more than a forgotten memento of the 1898 Spanish-American War.

Given the circumstances, Lino and his cabinet, consisting of his mother, Nereida, and former fellow students of his University political science classes, drafted a legislative proposal to President Okinawa. The bill was titled the "Puerto Rico Economic Self-Sufficiency Act" or PRESSA. The bill's primary stated purpose was to reduce federal spending in Puerto Rico. However, the other major objective under PRESSA was to ensure that no change in the Puerto Rican government would hurt the creation and continuation of Puerto Rico City.

Under PRESSA, the federal government would stop the sale of the land of Roosevelt Roads. All the land would be declared a special federal economic enterprise zone governed exclusively by a commission that would regulate Puerto Rico City. Puerto Rico City would be immune from Puerto Rican laws. Commissioners would be Puerto Rico residents, appointed by the U.S. president, charged with the non-partisan duty to create from private funds and operate faithfully America's first fiscally autonomous, energy independent and environmentally conscious, master-planned entertainment city. All net tax revenue from Puerto Rico City would be paid to the Puerto Rico government and reduce federal payments to the island on a dollar-per-dollar basis.

Okinawa called Lino and invited him to the White House. They held a joint press conference from the Rose Garden. Okinawa hailed PRESSA as "an innovative, job-creating initiative that would save the federal government billions of dollars each year while securing Puerto Rico's economic self-sufficiency."

The statehood and commonwealth parties launched media blitzes calling Lino "A traitor to his people."

A newspaper editorial read: "Does Governor Mendoza think that Puerto Ricans cannot do the job themselves? This proves that Puerto Rico City is a fantasy."

Lino responded by televised address.

"If we can't do the job, it's because the local parties will try to stop us. We need to get them out of our way. Under PRESSA, we will be able to build Puerto Rico City and not have the politicians trying to slice up the property to give favors to their friends and business partners.

"If you want independence from political parties, if you want to create your own futures, this is our chance."

Lino took a caravan of cars around the island and spoke from a megaphone in each city and town. The chants in favor of the insulated enterprise zone grew steadily until even the statehood and commonwealth party leaders stopped their campaigns against it.

However, on SNM and Box News, U.S. Senator Neckles and Congressman Spandeport denounced PRESSA as an "accounting trick" that would only perpetuate the "useless subsidies" that the U.S. had showered upon Puerto Rico, long after the island lost its strategic military value.

With his pink face and slitty eyes, Neckles stood on the steps of the U.S. Capitol with a copy of a bill rolled up in his hands. Spandeport approached the microphones with his jet black hair and outturned ears and said: "The time has come for Puerto Rico to enjoy full sovereignty."

He read a joint statement summarizing their proposed legislation:

"We see no reason for keeping Puerto Rico as a territory of the U.S. when it only costs us money. There is also no reason to offer statehood when Puerto Ricans have rejected statehood on at least three prior occasions. Three strikes and you're out.

"Since the U.S. closed Roosevelt Roads in 2004, we must admit that Puerto Rico's role as part of our nation is complete. We understand that Puerto Ricans have fought in every U.S. war since World War I. However, all parts of our country must carry their own weight. We cannot continue to subsidize an island that pays no federal taxes.

"As for Roosevelt Roads, the U.S. must leave entirely from Puerto Rico. The land on Roosevelt Roads will be sold, and the buyers may do as they wish without involving the federal government in any way.

"Therefore, we have submitted our own legislation, the Puerto Rico Independence Act, known as PRIA ('PRY-YA' was how he pronounced it), to give Puerto Rico its complete sovereignty. This is a fair solution to a political problem that has vexed both the U.S. and Puerto Rico for more than 100 years.

"The act also recognizes Puerto Ricans' contributions to our great nation. Puerto Ricans born before independence will retain their U.S. citizenship. Those born after the enactment will become citizens of Puerto Rico and will be treated as foreign nationals. Puerto Rico will then finally determine its own destiny."

Lino struggled to find a response to the compelling logic. The press release correctly referred to three local plebiscites in 1967, 1993 and 1998, which failed to achieve a majority in favor of statehood. He could quarrel with the assertion about federal taxes: Puerto Rico residents paid the full panoply of federal taxes, including federal income tax on their worldwide income and Social Security and Medicare taxes. There is only a limited exemption from federal taxes for income earned in Puerto Rico (known to tax buffs as "Puerto Rico-source income"). However, this nuance would be lost on most listeners.

President Okinawa announced that he would veto the Puerto Rico Independence Act. In retaliation, Neckles and Spandeport used procedural tactics to stop PRESSA from getting out of the congressional committee responsible for Puerto Rico affairs. Intriguingly, Neckles and Spandeport had initially supported PRESSA, but their party had united against Okinawa so that he could not claim credit for the slightest legislative achievement, no matter how sensible the legislation was on its merits.

Lino faulted himself for not having correctly played this card. He should have first gone to Neckles and Spandeport, especially since Lino was not officially conservative or liberal. Now it was too late. Midterm U.S. elections would eventually arrive. These could give Unicrats the two-thirds majority needed to override a presidential veto and enact the Puerto Rico Independence Act. Meanwhile, the U.S. Navy would be proceeding with the sale of Roosevelt Roads.

28 THE BORINQUEN TRUST

♦

Of course, being part of the United States was highly valuable to Puerto Rico City. If Puerto Rico became an independent nation, travel by U.S. citizens would require a passport and customs inspection on return to the U.S. Without free entrance and exit of the American traveler, an important competitive advantage of Puerto Rico City would be gone.

The last time that Puerto Rico faced a unilateral threat of independence was in 1936. Two members of a nationalist youth movement had assassinated the chief of police who, at the time, was a U.S. official. Then, it was anger and outrage behind the U.S. initiative to cut

Puerto Rico loose as an independent nation. These emotions dissipated steadily, however, when the two suspects were shot dead almost immediately after they were arrested. No trial, no jury, and instant retribution.

Now, however, there was no instant retribution to be had. Something far more transcendent and quintessentially American drove the idea of forced Puerto Rican independence: Money.

The Puerto Rican archipelago was simply too expensive to maintain without any offsetting benefits. Puerto Ricans could argue until they were purple-faced about their loyal military service to the U.S. However, PRIA (which Lino dubbed *la Piranha*) would address that problem by preserving U.S. citizenship for all Puerto Ricans born before independence and allowing them to immigrate freely to the U.S. The Puerto Rican lobby in the U.S. Congress had no cogent response to the cost-benefit analysis.

Neither did Lino. Yet, faced with this foreseeable threat, Lino reasoned that his idea to redirect Puerto Rico's economy was still sound. What else could Puerto Rico do to sustain itself? How could it compete in a global economy without adopting play-money currency and devaluing to peasant wages? Lino could think of no other place in the Americas planning a diversified mega-entertainment city in a tropical climate. Inbound traveler and customs inspections in Puerto Rico could be eliminated altogether. Hence, in visitors' minds, Puerto Rico would not be the irritant. It would be the U.S. Also, the four million Puerto Ricans living in the U.S. would continue to have family and emotional bonds that would bring them back as loyal tourists to the island. On the other hand, there was also the specter of doubt about the follow-through on the punitive legislation. Cutting Puerto Rico off from the U.S. could ignite a Hispanic American backlash against the Unicrats lasting for decades. Another major backfire was also possible: The passage of *la Piranha* could trigger a tsunami of Puerto Rican migration, engulfing the lily-white shores of the U.S. just before independence took full effect. Finally, Lino knew what Nereida would say about responding to the threat of forced independence: *"You can ask for a favor, but never, ever beg."*

Because of the controversy surrounding Puerto Rico's status, "Lino Mendoza, the governor of the beleaguered U.S. island territory," was in the national news. Drawing on his heightened profile, Lino called Burton Fletcher at Ashton & Cavendish.

"Governor Mendoza, I hear that Puerto Rico may be headed for new horizons and perhaps even fall off a cliff." Fletcher said.

"One might say that," said Lino. "It still hasn't happened though, and you know how unpredictable politics can be."

"True." Fletcher cleared his throat. "I also see that you made your mother the secretary of state. I hope it's really you and not her who is running the show."

"She still decides what I have for lunch, but she's perfectly capable of taking charge if necessary."

"Lino, you always cover all the bases. Tell me, governor, to what do I owe this high honor?"

"Well, on behalf of the People of Puerto Rico, I have a *pro bono* request."

"You know how much the firm hates those," Fletcher said.

"Just take this into consideration: The publicity for Ashton & Cavendish may be very valuable. Also, this might lead to paid legal work. At a minimum, I can recommend the firm. And the feds will provide us with money to pay for legal counsel just to make sure that cutting Puerto Rico off from its lifeline is done properly."

Fletcher would have hung up in mid-sentence if he wasn't the slightest bit interested.

Lino continued: "I want to set up a trust that will seek contributions from all natural born Puerto Ricans living in Puerto Rico. An intra-'commonwealth' stock offering ... great training for first and second-year corporate attorneys ... the Ashton & Cavendish name will prominently appear in public notices ... a worthy charitable cause in the name of economic and political self-determination."

Lino talked for about an hour with more details. Fletcher listened.

"Sounds intriguing. I'll take it to the management committee," Fletcher said.

Lino knew what that meant. So right after hanging up the phone, Lino went to the media. Then it was too late for Ashton & Cavendish to decline. In *The Wall Street Journal*, *The New York Times*, and *The Washington Post*, Lino effusively thanked the firm and Fletcher Burton personally for their generous support: "A firm so committed to the economic advancement and self-determination of the Puerto Rican people deserves everyone's respect and admiration," Lino said in his final sentence.

Then Lino gave a detailed speech, which appeared in the island television and radio stations and on the Internet:

"I am announcing the creation of the Borinquen Trust. Each share is $1,000. Natural born Puerto Ricans residing on the island may own a maximum of ten shares. Persons with income below $10,000 may purchase one-tenth of a share for one hundred dollars. The money will be used to buy Roosevelt Roads and to build Puerto Rico City. Each buyer must present a Puerto Rico birth certificate and proof of residency. Each share in the Borinquen Trust will be strictly a personal asset. It cannot be sold. Any unlawful purchase or sale will forfeit the purchase money to the fund. When an owner dies or moves from Puerto Rico, the share will automatically cancel and revert back to the fund. Shareholders will vote for the board, and the top executive officer will make no more than the salary of the governor of Puerto Rico. No one may serve on the board for more than six years. Profits, if they exist, will be paid each year. Therefore, the only way to make your share pay is to make Puerto Rico City work.

"My fellow Puerto Ricans, we must act now. I know that, for many of you, even one hundred dollars is a huge sacrifice and perhaps even beyond your reach. So I urge those who have had better fortunes to lend your fellow Puerto Ricans a hand. When each of us feels that we own a part of a common future, we will come together to do the work that's needed. With or without the United States, Puerto Rico must become self-reliant. There is no better plan than Puerto Rico City."

With 3.7 million Puerto Ricans living on the island, a full subscription of one share by all at the base price would bring in $3.7 billion, and even more if persons bought the ten-share maximum. In the first six weeks, more than two million Puerto Ricans either mailed in their contribution and qualifying papers or flooded the *colecturías* (government collection offices) across the island to purchase their investment. During the seventh and eighth weeks, about 100,000 payments of $10,000 each arrived. However, the proofs of residence were mainly clustered in Bayamón and Carolina, the municipalities to the west and east of San Juan. Lino ordered an investigation. The birth certificates received during those last two weeks were counterfeit. This had negative and positive consequences. On the downside, Puerto Rico had to create entirely new birth certificates with heightened security features. On the upside, the counterfeit birth certificates, creatively printed by rogue document technicians within the California Demographic Registry, were traced to Aaron Getz, who thought he could stay in the game somehow. As a result, he was named as defendant in New York and California federal indictments for mail and wire fraud. Better yet for the People of Puerto Rico, the Getz "contributions" were forfeited to the Borinquen Trust.

By the auction deadline, the Borinquen Trust had $3.2 billion. With the looming threat of Puerto Rico's independence, the Borinquen Trust bought the entire thirteen-square-mile landmass for $100 million, leaving $3.1 billion for improvements.

29 PUERTO RICO AIR

♦

Despite Lino's public requests to the contrary, the shareholders of the Borinquen Trust elected him as the chairman and chief executive officer of the fund. With the legal prohibition of a government official running the Borinquen Trust, Lino resigned his position as governor. By constitutional mandate, his mother Nereida succeeded him as the governor of Puerto Rico. The U.S. news media seized on these events as presaging Puerto Rico's future as an independent banana republic, prone to dictators, nepotism, and corruption.

These accusations were nothing new, Lino thought, and they were certainly not unique to Puerto Rico. Moreover, worse charges could be made up about individual states of the United States. Lino forged ahead with his plans. He set up the offices of the Borinquen Trust in the former NCO club on Roosevelt Roads. He hired a staff of young, attractive college women from the University of Puerto Rico. He changed all the entrances to read "Puerto Rico City." As Puerto Rico City's chief proponent, he would have to look the part. He lifted weights in the morning and laid out in the afternoon to build up a tan. He dressed in white. He made all public event appearances flanked each time by a half dozen show-stopping Puerto Rican women. Several Puerto Rico City women were spirited away for modeling and acting contracts. Yet there was a rushing stream of new volunteers. Lino's staff would publish notices on the website, and women appeared for casting calls by the hundreds. Even one appearance as a Puerto Rico City woman would give lifetime bragging rights.

The first major construction project was to build out the Puerto Rico City airport. Most of the $3 billion would go here. The airport would use both runways. He hired architects and contractors to design and build terminals that could receive at least 15,000 passengers per day, about one Boeing 757 with 200 passengers landing six times an hour, twelve hours per day. Lino then published requests for proposals to start Puerto

Rico Air, which would have priority rights to use gates at the Puerto Rico City airport. Private jets could fly to the former Fajardo municipal airport after extending its runway.

Next, he worked with urban planners to layout the city and its rail transportation system. The shuttle train would start at the airport and stop at twelve primary locations along the north and south ends of the three-mile horseshoe bay. The urban planners designed 15 sites ranging from 50 to 300 acres each for the city's primary hotel-casino resorts and sports and performing arts arenas. *El Boriqwalk*, the Puerto Rico City promenade, would be lined by palm and flamboyan trees and have towers spraying cooling mist every 50 yards. Waste receptacles would appear just as often and smiling beautification associates would patrol in white gloves to ensure spotlessness.

Puerto Rico City published international invitations for ground lease concessions for each of the 15 major sites. Each site was to be operated by a separate firm with no interlocking ownership. Competitive tension between owners was critical. Ground leases would last 50 to 75 years, provided that a minimum number of hotel rooms were built. The more rooms, the longer the lease. Lease payments were two percent of the gross revenues plus 20 percent of profits – similar to what major hedge fund managers charged for assets under management. The two percent component would be reinvested in infrastructure and maintenance.

And no, there were no tax break giveaways.

With stunning Puerto Rico City beauty queens at his side (the "Honor Guard" as he later called them), Lino appeared in commercials and televised interviews in New York, London, Paris, Buenos Aires, Cape Town, Mumbai, Sidney, Tokyo, and Shanghai. In Riyadh, the capital of Saudi Arabia, Lino stressed "virgin" beverages and the numerous non-gaming activities, deep sea fishing, snorkeling, golfing, tennis, hiking, and horseback riding. (Eyes rolled and the audience wanted to know more about the liquor supply chain, betting limits and dance shows).

Despite the political uncertainty caused by the independence bills pending in the U.S. Congress, the invitations were oversubscribed in just few months. There was simply no other opportunity like this in the Western Hemisphere. Construction began on seven of the sites to build 20,000 new hotel rooms, casinos and performance arenas. On each end of the harbor, the first two anchor properties with 4,000 hotel rooms each were the Cariblux Palace and the Quixote Castle. News that $20 billion had been committed to Puerto Rico City appeared in U.S. and international television and business newspapers.

Then, while other major U.S. airlines boasted stellar profits, American Airways filed for bankruptcy. After Lino went to the media with the idea, a group of private investors saw the opportunity and bought more than fifty of its jets. They started Puerto Rico Air. The new airline purchased priority gate assignments for the Puerto Rico City airport from the Borinquen Trust. In the shadow of Puerto Rico's forced independence, Puerto Rico Air requested and received certain exemptions from federal law. Planes contained a first-class section, a business section, a section for minors and their parents, a gaming cabin and the adult section (more expensive than first class and always overbooked).

Before anyone boarded, flight attendants stowed carry-on luggage above the passengers' actual assigned seats. Boarding started for those seated in the rear of the plane, reducing bottlenecks in the aisles and the time needed to fill the plane. Restless first-class passengers sat cool and pretty in their own ritzy section of the Puerto Rico Air hospitality lounge. Other parts of the "PRAir" hospitality lounge featured salsa and merengue lessons with blazing-hot instructors. There were pre-boarding and onboard massages. Flight attendants sported tropical beachwear while offering duty-free items, including Don Collins, Don Pedro and Boriqua Puro cigars. Wi-Fi was always included in the ticket price. Peanuts and pretzels? No way. Plantain chips, *alcapurrias* and *pastelillos,* exquisite fritter dishes putting calamari to shame. The airplane galleys were equipped to serve *piña coladas, mojitos,* and *daiquiris*.

While perhaps lacking the geopolitical urgency of the Berlin Airlift, the Puerto Rico City airlift was just as vital. Last-minute passengers, rapidly becoming the norm on weekends, could buy tickets at departure kiosks. During the flight, passengers could book rooms, events, and restaurant reservations. Ticket prices were dynamically discounted by Puerto Rico hotel, restaurant and event bookings, even on board. Copies of *Puerto Rico City News* gave a day-by-day rundown of sites and happenings. With a legal drinking age of 18, Puerto Rico became synonymous with Spring Break.

Welcoming music at the Puerto Rico City airport featured young reggaeton and salsa hip-hop bands cutting their teeth on newcomer audiences. Passengers rode sleek shuttle trains to their hotels that arrived in a matter of minutes. Wasting timed standing in line for a taxi or at a rental car company became an obsolete concept.

Departure gifts by Puerto Rico City women and men included tropical sweets: *ajonjolí* (sesame seed candy), *mampostial* (coconut caramel), and *dulce de batata* (sweet potato candy) with a Puerto Rican good fortune message, such as: "A good thing happened to you, and you will remember it forever."

30 STATESIDE CRUCIBLE

The Unicrats swept the congressional midterm elections, taking two-thirds control of both the U.S. Senate and House of Representatives. This meant that, voting as a block, the Unicrats could override any veto by President Okinawa. Neckles and Spandeport reintroduced new bills in both chambers of Congress to make Puerto Rico an independent country.

President Okinawa threatened to veto the bills, but a veto would only delay passage while the same Congress was convened. Even then, Okinawa had larger battles to fight. Unicratic proposals to eliminate Geria-Care and Mendi-Caid, the government-sponsored health insurance programs for the elderly and poor, crept through both houses of Congress.

Curt Calloustone, a Unicratic senator from Iowa, proposed that the retired elderly receive a voucher to buy private health insurance. Presumably, the voucher would be enough to purchase health insurance that seniors had not been able to afford or obtain when they were twenty years younger and still working. Cost-cutting proposals to help the poor focused on taking them to the steps of churches and synagogues. Unicrats then rolled out cuts to education and environmental protection. They also wanted to stop the repair of the nation's highways, bridges, airports and seaports. A broadband system behind South Korea's was no concern. The premise was that the U.S. would be better off if Americans were less educated, the country dirtier, the transportation infrastructure in tatters, and the communications system second rate.

Despite the exploding national debt, Calloustone and the Unicrats also called for lower tax rates "to unleash America's economic potential." Okinawa's predecessor had already reduced the top marginal rate from 39.6 percent to 35 percent. After the tax cuts, in order to make up for the lost revenue, the taxable real GDP would have had to grow each year by about 12 percent. The last time real GDP grew by more than 12 percent was in 1942, 1943 and 1944 during the height of World War II. Ironically, in those years, the top marginal tax rates ranged from 88 percent to 94 percent, and these rates evidently did not deter American businesses. Now, after the tax cuts, instead of the GDP growing, the financial crisis struck and, for the first time in decades, the U.S. economy shrank.

Finally, another initiative sought economic growth by reducing the U.S. population through mass deportations of millions of undocumented aliens, mostly Hispanics. After being so instrumental in bringing down the Berlin Wall, the world's champion of personal freedom and human mobility would seal the southern border with unmanned aerial vehicles and a double-layer fence with razor edges – "the guillotine" as some called it.

In all fairness, from time to time, counter-intuitive ideas, à-la-smallpox vaccine, had advanced mankind and increased the general welfare. Only time could tell if these would work, although any possible configuration of Calloustone, Neckles and Spandeport bore no resemblance to Edward Jenner.

The austerity crusade marched on in Congress. Senator Calloustone's larger cost-cutting bills in health, education, environmental protection and transportation received priority. His front-runner status as the Unicratic candidate for the 2012 elections leapfrogged his measures ahead of those of Neckles and Spandeport.

Calloustone was a corn-and-milk darling of the Unicratic Party. Square-jawed, blond and tall, he had a wife and four children. He went to church on Sunday and rose in political stature on the apparent consistency of his family values and "faith-based" agenda. Although his father had been born in Mexico to American missionaries, he was staunchly anti-immigrant. He led the Senate by blocking every legislative initiative by President Okinawa. While Calloustone took seven years to graduate with a college degree in business from Tar Sands State University, he was virtually dictating the nation's fiscal policy.

In essence, to stop the world's largest economy from collapsing, the government had to protect the vast fortunes of the rich from higher taxes and government investments. Furthermore, banks and financial institutions that played key roles in precipitating the financial crisis should continue to do business unfettered by regulation. The free market was sacrosanct, and its God-like invisible hand would protect us all. Unless it concerned immigration by Hispanics, unwanted pregnancies, human sexual orientation or personal drug use, any government intrusion was a heretical idea. Evolution was a hoax. And it was absurd to suggest that industrial pollution could contribute to global warming. The U.S. should continue to reduce taxes, but its military would remain the world's most powerful.

To boost his presidential prospects, Calloustone's party acted first on his deregulation and tax-cutting bills, approving them and sending them to President Okinawa. Okinawa vetoed them, but under the U.S. Constitution, the vetoed bills returned to Congress, which then held another vote and passed them with a two-third's majority over the president's veto. Despite lower taxes and less regulation, the American economy continued to slide.

Before the U.S. presidential election of 2012, unemployment was raging to heights not seen since the Great Depression. As the human oceans brimmed with jobless bodies, the supply of cheap labor ballooned. Corporate executives were earning more than three hundred times the average wage of their employees. Although food stamp recipients multiplied, manufacturers of private jets and yachts had record backlogs in their order books. Congress rejected legislation that would force foreign banks with U.S. branches to disclose the identities of American depositors that held secret accounts in their countries. (Instead, accountholder disclosure "requests" would be channeled only through the foreign governments "to reduce compliance costs and prevent violations of the foreign privacy laws"). Trillions of dollars of company profits were salted away overseas where they would never be taxed. Nonetheless, when U.S. companies' foreign operations ran into trouble, when their intellectual property was infringed by the Chinese, when their vessels commandeered by Somali pirates, or when one of their executives was wrongfully detained by Indian police, all went running to the U.S. government for help. While dodging taxes abroad, the Earth's most protected citizens demanded the costly deployment of treaties, embassies, diplomats, courts, the military, and other resources maintained around the world by the U.S. government.

As Calloustone promised still lower taxes and less regulation, U.S. and foreign corporations exercised their constitutional right to free speech by pouring hundreds of millions into campaign "documentaries" bashing Okinawa. The voices of these constitutionally recognized "persons" with no right to vote (at least not yet) did the job.

On November 6, 2012, Okinawa lost the presidential election to Calloustone.

On January 2, 2013, the last day of a lame duck Congress, President Okinawa received the Puerto Rico Independence Act, which had been delayed by the election-year frenzy. Normally, the president must object to legislation within ten days or the bill becomes law. Since Okinawa's presidency expired on January 20, 2013 and since a new Congress would have to convene, Okinawa did nothing and used a pocket veto. A new bill would have to be submitted to the incoming new Congress. In any event, when the new Congress convened on January 3, they did so only to change the carpeting, install more comfortable seating, and upgrade the wireless system of the Capitol for faster Internet surfing. Several Congressmen, even some from Okinawa's party, were seen checking Facebook and playing online computer games.

As provided by the Constitution, at noon, January 20, 2013, Calloustone was inaugurated as president of the United States. His inauguration speech stressed the importance of "living within one's means" and that "the government is the problem and should step out of the way." The Dow Jones and S&P plunged 20 percent during the new president's first three trading days in office. Military tensions with Iran rose again in Strait of Hormuz. After claiming that it had only one aircraft carrier (a training vessel, as it were), China launched three carriers in the South China Sea.

With lower tax revenues and its raging national debt, the U.S. started the year by delaying payments to armed forces personnel.

31 THE CITY

In 2013, the Puerto Rico City airport, the rail system and ten resorts were complete. Of the total 32,000 new rooms, 25,000 were finished and booked solid, mostly with recession-resistant U.S. patrons who lived largely on dividends and capital gains. Meanwhile, the construction of seven additional hotels was furiously underway. Puerto Rico Air landed every few minutes. The airports in San Juan and Aguadilla had to service overflow traffic. Passengers landing in San Juan spent a few days there, then took the new twenty-five minute train to Puerto Rico City. Those arriving in Aguadilla drove the scenic ride along the north coast, visited the beaches, the Camuy caverns, the Arecibo radio telescope. Then they made their way to San Juan and eventually to Puerto Rico City.

The Puerto Rico City sports pavilion seating 60,000 had opened, and the first scheduled event was a world title boxing match between Marty Packiton and Foy Merriman.

Major League Baseball expanded with the Puerto Rico City Sharks in the National League. Their opening day game would be against the New York Yankees, and Lino would be throwing out the first pitch.

Puerto Rico winter league baseball, which in the 1950s and 60s had featured Hall of Famers Roberto Clemente, Willie Mays, Orlando Cepeda and Hank Aaron, roared back to life. Started in 1938, the league had dwindled to just four teams. Now there were eight. With its superior glitz, Puerto Rico City's team led the way. Other teams filled stadiums in San Juan, Carolina, Bayamón, Ponce, Aguadilla, Arecibo, and Mayagüez. Major League Baseball players, who had coasted and gotten flabby during the off season, now competed for a winter team spot and the best island real estate to go with it.

Youth baseball academies in the Dominican Republic started losing market share of major league talent scouts and recruiters to Puerto Rico. At their first opportunity, young Cuban baseball refugees moved to Puerto Rico.

Racehorse owners from the Middle East, officially with no interest in betting, air-freighted their thoroughbreds and ran them with island jockeys. The Camarero Race Track, a few miles west of Puerto Rico City, required a major expansion to accommodate the spectators. The Puerto Rico Triple Crown, rescheduled to start in July, drew U.S. riders and their mounts who were rested up after the Kentucky Derby, the Preakness, and the Belmont Stakes.

Lyon Irons made his professional golf comeback by winning the Puerto Rico City Cup championship. With this win, Irons broke a multi-year slump after his ex-wife had battered him with a three wood and ran off with half of his fortune and her personal trainer. He and other golf professionals from Europe and South Africa bought homes in Puerto Rico for year-round practice on the island's courses.

Meanwhile, international concert stars such as Lowe Jay, Marcus Antonious, Rod Markin and Bitten Pull had signed multi-year contracts to perform at the Cariblux Palace, the Quixote Castle, the Armada, and El Huracán. Yachts owned by the Sultan of Brunei, the

Saudi royals, and Mikhail Petrovich, the Russian oil and gas oligarch still on the lookout for Sergei Rubelkov, were regularly docked in the Puerto Rico City harbor.

Although her indictment was still pending, there were reports that a woman resembling Daisy Youngluck had arrived by a private jet in the Fajardo municipal airport, spent a few hours at the baccarat tables at the Cariblux Palace, then slipped away the same way she came. An investment fund secretly owned by Wen Kashing tried to bid on a casino resort concession, but a due diligence investigation uncovered Wen's involvement and stopped it.

A battalion of defense lawyers unloaded an avalanche of records and assembled parades of witnesses that distanced Getz from the birth certificate counterfeiters. Without admitting or denying any wrongdoing, Getz paid the federal government $200 million in exchange for a deferred prosecution agreement conditioned upon his never returning to Puerto Rico. With his abortive dates, Getz would visit anyway, wagering – again – that camels pass through the eye of a needle more often than the rich go to heaven or jail.

Paparazzi found fertile ground for celebrity sightings. Film crews and movie stars were regular visitors. Two Puerto Rican international celebrities, who had recently and inexplicably become citizens of Spain, renounced their expatriate plans and returned to Puerto Rico. U.S. and world political figures were seen on *El Boriqwalk*, the Puerto Rico City promenade. Even Senator Neckles and Congressmen Spandeport were spotted. *The New York Times* and *Financial Times* published a photograph of them clinking *piña coladas* with lobbyists on a private boat headed from the Puerto Rico City harbor to the bioluminescent bay in Vieques. Reporters quoted Neckles saying, "Yes, Puerto Rico still belongs to the United States." Another report in *The Wall Street Journal* appeared with the headline: "U.S. Losing Billions in Taxes from Puerto Rico City."

Puerto Rico's unemployment had dropped from 16 percent to less than 4 percent. The first dividend payment for each full share of the Borinquen Trust was $3,000, triple the initial investment.

32 STATEHOOD

President Calloustone sat in the Oval Office. He had been in the White House for almost a year. He ran his hand through the top of his blond hair as he read the news about America's continuing descent. One of the few bright spots was the island territory that the country had been planning to cast off.

Calloustone called Neckles and Spandeport. "Gentlemen, does this still make sense?" They talked and talked again for weeks, then months.

***

In the governor's study next to a small kitchen in the north wing of La Fortaleza, Governor Nereida Mendoza told her assistant that he could go home for lunch. Lino was visiting Old San Juan for the day. More than a year ago, Nereida had been inaugurated for a second term as governor of Puerto Rico. Lino came into the governor's study with copies of several national and international newspapers. Nereida went into the kitchen and began cooking rice, sweet plantains and steak for her son.

Lino read the news that President Calloustone had presented a statehood bill to Congress.

"Never," Lino said.

"What did you say?" his mother asked from the kitchen.

"I said, never, Mom. I said never."

ABOUT THE AUTHOR

David R. Martin was born in Toledo, Ohio. He studied literature, history and economics at Amherst College and law in Puerto Rico and New York. He enjoys playing blackjack and warm weather. He lives in Atlanta, Georgia.

For more about the author, visit www.puertoricocity.com.